"Unless you marry me as planned, Max," Lavinia threatened, *"I'll*  *about y*

"What scandal He was truly baffled.

"Let's just say that before my mother died," Lavinia replied coldly, "she told me a secret about your family, Max. Something terrible. Something that would destroy all of you, but mostly your beloved little brat of a sister, Sarah. That's all I'll say. Push me, and all of England will know the story. That's the very reason Mum told me the secret in the first place. As a sort of security system, just in case I'd need it to get what I want. And what I want is for our wedding to go on, as expected."

With that, the duchess stood and walked gracefully from the room.

What is she talking about? Max wondered.

A chill ran up his spine as he stared at her departing figure. He rose to call her back, but he found himself speechless.

Bantam Books in the Elizabeth series.
Ask your bookseller for the books you have missed.

Visit the Official Sweet Valley Web Site on the Internet at:
www.sweetvalley.com

Elizabeth

Max's Choice

WRITTEN BY
LAURIE JOHN

CREATED BY
FRANCINE PASCAL

BANTAM BOOKS
NEW YORK·TORONTO·LONDON·SYDNEY·AUCKLAND

RL: 8, AGES 014 AND UP

MAX'S CHOICE

A Bantam Book / May 2001

Sweet Valley High® *and Sweet Valley University*®
are registered trademarks of Francine Pascal.
Elizabeth is a trademark owned by Francine Pascal.
Conceived by Francine Pascal.

Copyright © 2001 by Francine Pascal.
Cover art copyright © 2001 by Mark Stuwe/Arts Counsel

Produced by 17th Street Productions,
an Alloy Online, Inc. company.
33 West 17th Street
New York, NY 10011.

ISBN: 0-553-49357-4

Visit us on the Web! www.randomhouse.com/teens

Published simultaneously in the United States and Canada

Bantam Books is an imprint of Random House Children's Books, a division
of Random House, Inc. BANTAM BOOKS and the rooster colophon are
registered trademarks of Random House, Inc. Bantam Books, 1540
Broadway, New York, New York 10036.

PRINTED IN THE UNITED STATES OF AMERICA

OPM   0 9 8 7 6 5 4 3 2 1

To Anders Johansson

Chapter One

"A little more muscle with that silver polish, Vanessa!"

Elizabeth Wakefield glanced up from her own task as her boss, Mary Dale, the head housekeeper of Pennington House, swept into the kitchen and glared at the other maid. Mary was no-nonsense as usual. Vanessa rolled her eyes, also as usual.

The heavyset, middle-aged woman glanced everywhere at once, making sure her worker bees were busy. "The earl took care to mention that there was a touch of tarnish on the dinner service, Vanessa, and you know how particular he is about the family plate." Mary paused to take a taste from one of the pots simmering on the stove. "This will do," she directed to no one in particular since Cook wasn't in the room at the moment. "And Elizabeth," Mary continued. "When you're done mopping the floor, sweep up underneath the dining-room table. Sarah broke a glass." At Elizabeth's nod, Mary strode out of the kitchen.

Elizabeth wrung out the mop. After almost five months at Pennington House she knew how to deal with small mishaps like broken glass, she knew to address the earl respectfully, she knew how to make beds so that you could bounce a quarter off the sheets, and she knew how to mop a mean floor.

In fact, when all was said and done, she had to admit that she'd learned a lot of useful things since she'd come to England. Well, useful for a maid in England, that was.

Still, she couldn't help feeling bemused at the skills she'd picked up. Less than a year ago she wouldn't have known the difference between an ice cream fork and a fish fork; now she knew exactly how to place them on the table and how to fold a napkin to look like a tulip. *Who even knew that there were such things as ice cream forks?* Elizabeth shook her head as she swiped the mop over the ancient stone floor. *And who would have ever thought that I'd end up as a kitchen maid to the earl of Pennington?*

Elizabeth closed her eyes for a moment as she

thought of the incredible odyssey that had brought her to this point, halfway around the world, separated from her family, toiling as a servant under an assumed name, and living in an attic with two other maids.

Was it really only five months ago since she'd fled to England at night, leaving her parents openmouthed behind her in the Chicago airport? Elizabeth stopped mopping and leaned against the wall. Her eyes were focused on Vanessa as she polished the silver, but her mind was far away, back at the O'Hare airport on that fateful night.

I'd never been so mad or hurt in all my life, Elizabeth recalled, sighing as she remembered the angry scene. Her parents had been furious with her and demanded that she come home with them, but Elizabeth had vowed that she'd never go home, she'd never go home as long as Jessica was there because as far as Elizabeth was concerned, Jessica was no longer her sister. She'd stopped being her sister the moment that Elizabeth had caught her in her boyfriend's arms.

Ex-boyfriend.

Elizabeth and her Sam, along with her sister, Jessica, and *her* boyfriend, Tyler, had been on a cross-country summer road trip. Things had been going well, or so she had thought. No, things had apparently been going well between Jessica and Sam.

How could my own sister steal my boyfriend? Elizabeth frowned as she resumed her attack on the floor. At least she could think of that night without wanting to cry. Now, when she thought of Sam and Jessica's treachery, she felt nothing more than a dull ache.

I guess that must be major progress, Elizabeth thought, pausing to tuck a strand of long, blond hair back into her ponytail. *When I first found them, I was ready to kill!*

Elizabeth had known—the second she'd seen Sam and Jessica locked in a passionate embrace—that her life as she knew it was finished. She hadn't been able to bear the thought of going home, back to Sweet Valley University, where she would surely run into them constantly. There was only one thing she *could* do. She could go to London.

Shortly before she'd left on that fateful road trip, Elizabeth had applied to the University of London for a semester-abroad program in creative writing. Elizabeth had been shocked when she'd received the acceptance letter and a scholarship; she hadn't been sure she wanted to leave her new relationship with Sam behind. But her feelings changed once she'd seen Sam and

Jessica. As far as she was concerned, she couldn't get to London and her new university fast enough.

She'd arrived in London without a clue about English culture, money, the rail system, or the unexpected language differences, plus she'd been nearly penniless and without the right clothes for damp, cool English weather. *But I didn't care,* Elizabeth thought as she mopped underneath the table, trying to avoid Vanessa's feet. *I was just so happy to be away from the United States. Away from California, Sweet Valley, my parents, who hadn't understood me at all, and, of course, away from my sister, who I'd vowed never to forgive.*

But a nasty surprise had been in store for her when she'd arrived at the University of London. Because she hadn't responded to their acceptance letter in time, the school had given her place to someone else. And suddenly Elizabeth Wakefield was in a foreign country with no friends, no money, no idea where to go, and without a good relationship with her parents. There had been no calling the Wakefields collect and begging for help.

And so Elizabeth had spent the day wandering in the rain, trying to find shelter and considering what to do. Finally, just as she was wondering whether she'd have to spend the night on a bench, she'd ended up outside Pennington House, which she mistook for a bed-and-breakfast. Amazingly enough, considering the luck she'd been having, Pennington House was looking for a new kitchen maid (the job came with room, board, and semi-decent pay), and Elizabeth Wakefield had been in the right place at the right time.

Elizabeth Bennet, that is, she mentally corrected herself, smiling as she sloshed the soapy water across the floor. Elizabeth had been afraid that if she gave her real last name, her parents would somehow be able to track her down and force her back home. So for all intents and purposes, Elizabeth Wakefield was no more. Everyone at Pennington House thought her name was Elizabeth Bennet, just like the heroine in her favorite book, *Pride and Prejudice*.

"Anyone for a cup of tea?" Matilda Kippers, the cook, breezed into the room, carrying the remains of the high tea that the earl and his sixteen-year-old daughter, Sarah, had just finished. "I'm ready for a break."

Elizabeth smiled gratefully. "I'd love one." She finished mopping the floor and sat down for a second at the large table in the center of the room. "How about you, Vanessa?" she asked. "Have some tea with us?"

6

Vanessa shrugged noncommittally as she polished the silver, and Elizabeth couldn't help sighing. Vanessa wasn't exactly the easiest person to deal with. When Elizabeth had first arrived, Vanessa had been downright nasty. There were times, however, when it seemed like she and Vanessa might be able to get along. A month ago there had been a misunderstanding that had almost resulted in Elizabeth being fired, and surprisingly enough, Vanessa had come staunchly to her defense, and they'd bonded a little bit. Since then, though—nothing.

Elizabeth wished that they could talk, really talk, especially because Elizabeth hadn't communicated with her family or friends back in Sweet Valley in the entire time that she'd been gone. She was badly in need of a confidant. She was badly in need of a friend.

"Here you are," Matilda said, placing a steaming cup of tea in front of Elizabeth and then sitting down opposite her. "If you fetch me a cloth, Vanessa, I'll lend a hand with that mountain of silver. I like doing mindless work while I rest."

"Mindless is right," Vanessa muttered, tossing Cook a cloth.

"This tea is delicious," Elizabeth murmured. "Thank you." She smiled at Matilda as she added cream and sugar. *That's something else I've learned*

7

since being here! Elizabeth recalled. She'd shocked the kitchen staff originally by asking for coffee in the mornings. Coffee, let alone American style, wasn't exactly a British staple. There wasn't a Starbucks down the block either.

"Well," Matilda said as she began polishing the silver vigorously. "You girls are in for a bit of a treat round 'ere."

"I'm sure," Vanessa said, rolling her catlike almond eyes. "As if a treat is possible. Oh, wait a minute. Did the earl and his insufferable children get locked in a closet or stuck in some lift at the palace or something? Those are the only possible treats I can think of." Vanessa threw her cloth down on the table and leaned back to stretch her arms over her head.

"Shush, girl! Someone'll hear you!" Cook snapped, glaring at Vanessa as she glanced toward the door, which led to an impressive foyer between the front door and the massive marble stairway. It wasn't often that any of the Penningtons actually came into the kitchen, but who knew who might be just outside the door in listening distance, zippering up a jacket or tying a scarf snugly. "The treat is that Mary says we can all have the rest of the day off."

"What about dinner?" Elizabeth frowned. "Who's going to serve dinner?"

8

"The earl is dining out," Matilda replied between sips of tea. "And apparently Sarah will be out with Max."

Max! Elizabeth nearly dropped her cup. Was Max coming home? She hadn't seen him in weeks!

Max Pennington, the earl's son, was twenty-one and drop-dead gorgeous. Elizabeth had fallen for him—hard. Which wouldn't have been a problem except that she was a scullery maid and Max was a noble. They cared about things like that in England. A lot. *Oh, and one other thing just so happens to be standing in our way,* Elizabeth thought sadly as she finished the rest of her tea. *Max is getting married in just a month!*

Elizabeth knew that she was smart, but for a smart girl, she made some amazingly stupid choices in guys. *I mean, first I pick Sam, who goes after my own sister, and then I pick Max, who's already gone after someone else! A duchess, no less!*

But it wasn't as if she had *picked* Max to fall in love with; it just sort of happened. There was a chemistry between them that couldn't be denied. *At least I think there is.* Elizabeth sighed. She was sure that Max felt the same way about her—he'd kissed her, hadn't he? It had been wrong; they both knew it. But they hadn't been able to help it. The kiss has happened.

Yeah, but that was a month ago, Elizabeth thought as she ran her fingers across her mouth. Her lips tingled as she remembered. He'd told her that he cared for her, but he'd also told her that his duty to his family—and by extension, his fiancée—was more important to him than his own feelings. He didn't love the duchess. He didn't. Elizabeth knew it. He was marrying her out of a sense of allegiance to his father because two powerful English families needed to be united, blah blah blah. Elizabeth didn't get it. Well, she did, sort of. But she'd never understand how anyone could marry someone he or she didn't love.

Elizabeth wished that she could talk to Max again, but he'd been staying at the dorms in Oxford, working on a difficult section of his thesis with his study group. Or so he'd said. Perhaps he was staying at Oxford to avoid temptation. *Stop it!* Elizabeth yelled at herself. *How dare you be so selfish! The guy is engaged to someone else. How dare you try to come between them? How dare you hope he chooses you! You don't even sound like yourself!*

Because I've changed, she thought. *I have. I'm not the passive girl I used to be. I'm a fighter. And*

I've learned I can survive anything. But I've also learned I don't have to go down without a fight. And I want Max!

Right, Liz. Like he'd really choose you, a common kitchen maid, over a stunningly beautiful duchess named Lavinia, who probably bathes in champagne and is dripping with class.

Still, if only she could see Max, if only she could remind him that there was something very special between them. If only. *Stop it!* she told herself again. *Respect his choice. He was avoiding you for a reason. You have to respect his choice.*

And she'd also better respect the fact that maybe he *wasn't* avoiding her. Maybe he just didn't care. Maybe he had forgotten all about her?

If only I could talk to someone about what's going on! Elizabeth looked hopefully at Vanessa, who was busy sipping her own cup of tea. She looked considerably perkier since hearing that they had the rest of the day off, and Elizabeth figured that Vanessa might be into talking. *I might as well try,* she thought, smiling tentatively at her coworker. *It's not as if I have anyone else to talk to!*

"So do you think you might head into London?" Elizabeth asked. Pennington House was a private estate, on the outskirts of the city. If Vanessa was going to London, maybe she would join her.

"Dunno." Vanessa's brown eyes glinted mysteriously. "I might, but I might have other plans as well."

"Um." Elizabeth nodded. She had a strong feeling that Vanessa was thinking more about seeing James Leer, Max's best friend, than London. Elizabeth was sure that something was going on between the two of them. James was clearly in love with Vanessa, but it was hard to tell what Vanessa's feelings were. She didn't exactly confide in Elizabeth.

If only Max would take his cues from his best friend! Granted, James wasn't of noble birth, but he certainly hobnobbed with the upper crust of London society. If a kitchen maid was good enough for James Leer, why not for Max?

It's not that you're not good enough, Elizabeth, she corrected herself. *That has nothing to do with it. He owes his loyalty to his father, to his family.* Would she ever be able to accept what Max was doing? She didn't know.

"Well, maybe the two of us could go shopping or just walk around or whatever," Elizabeth began slowly. "That is, if you aren't doing something with James. . . ."

"James?" Vanessa glared at Elizabeth. "Whatever would make you think that I was doing something with that fop?"

"Well, I . . . I don't know, he seems pretty interested in you. . . ." Elizabeth trailed off.

"Just because he's interested in me doesn't mean that I return the compliment," Vanessa said tartly. She finished her tea and pushed back her chair. "I'm off."

Guess we won't be doing the town together, Elizabeth thought, feeling a bit rejected. She should be used to Vanessa by now. She stood up and took her cup over to the restaurant-sized dishwasher.

Well, she had the rest of the evening off and nothing to do. *So what?* Elizabeth shrugged. Maybe she'd go into London by herself, or maybe she'd just stay up in the attic and read a book. But Elizabeth knew what she'd really do with her free time. She'd do the same thing that she did the rest of the time, whether she was sweeping the floor or serving dinner. She'd daydream about Max.

"That's a super jumper, Vic."

Sarah Pennington leaned back against the headboard of her bed and critically eyed her best friend's outfit. Victoria looked terrific in one of Voyage's newest finds—a cropped cashmere cardigan embroidered with velvet flowers.

Both girls were students at the exclusive

13

Welles School and as such spent five days a week in what Sarah considered to be a perfectly hideous uniform. Sarah often tried to individualize her uniform as much as possible, but she was pretty limited as to what she could do. On the weekends, however, she was free to indulge her fashion sense as much as she wished, and indulge it she did. Today she was wearing a Bloody Young Blokes concert T-shirt (the bottom cropped to show a hint of tummy, of course) with a slim, black leather skirt and her funky new knee-high platform boots. Sarah got up and wandered over to the venetian gilt mirror that hung on the opposite wall. She tossed her long, light brown hair over her shoulder and studied her reflection. "Do you think I should crop this shirt a bit shorter, show my belly button?"

"Mmmm." Victoria nodded absentmindedly. "If you want your father or even your brother to ground you for another two weeks." Victoria continued flipping through the latest issue of *Jump!* "Omigod!" she yelled, using her favorite American expression.

"What?" Sarah asked, hoping Victoria wasn't going to remind her any more of the torture of having been grounded for two whole weeks. Her brother had grounded her, and even though he hadn't been around these past weeks, he'd sicced their horrible, eagle-eyed priss of a housekeeper on her to watch her every move.

"This—" Victoria held up the magazine so that Sarah could see the glossy double-page spread.

"Yum, yum, yum . . . ," Sarah breathed, staring at the pages. "Yes, indeed, definitely fanciable!" Sarah took the magazine from Victoria and sat on the arm of the chair. The magazine had a photo spread on the hot new pop-rock band Bloody Young Blokes, which was Sarah's current favorite. She'd already been to three of their concerts, and in fact, she was going to her fourth tonight, which was why she was wearing the shirt. She couldn't take her eyes off the photos of their lead singer, Bones McCall. Even in still photographs, he managed to give off a dark intensity that almost singed the page. He was so incredibly hot!

"They say he's going to be starting at Welles," Victoria informed her as she peered over Sarah's shoulder.

"Bosh!" Sarah exclaimed. "Impossible!" She scanned the contents of the article.

Bones McCall, the ultrahot sixteen-year-old lead singer of Bloody Young Blokes, will soon be attending the exclusive Welles School. For all those lucky Welles students, we can only say that we're green with envy. Trust us, girls, this bloke is hot!

"He certainly is," Sarah murmured, taking in his broad shoulders, shock of thick, sandy-blond hair, and smoldering dark blue eyes. "I think I might have to snare him."

"Good luck." Victoria took the magazine back. "I hear that Phillipa Ainsley has her claws well into him."

"Phillipa?" Sarah made a face. "You can't be serious! She's a cow!" Sarah knew Lady Phillipa—in the way that all the nobility knew everyone else—and she didn't like her very much. In fact, at school or whenever they got stuck at some society function, Phillipa was snotty. Well, so was Sarah. But Phillipa was snotty first.

If Philly Ainsley *was* dating Bones McCall, it would be a pleasure to take him away from her. "Well, I don't care if she does have her claws in him," Sarah exclaimed. "I'll snare him anyway!"

"Hmmm." Victoria raised an eyebrow as she studied the fashion pages. "I thought you were off boys these days."

"Maybe not." Sarah shrugged happily. It was true that she'd had a couple of disastrous interludes with members of the opposite sex lately, but that didn't mean she had to give them up forever, did it? "Fancy a bit of shopping?" Sarah cocked her head. "I think a new perfect outfit or two might just be the thing to help snag Bones." Sarah walked over to the enormous walk-in closet—it had been converted from an extra bedroom—and began rifling through her clothes. She had so many, but there was nothing here worthy of a rock-star snagging.

"But you don't have time before the concert," Victoria said, hanging her feet over the edge of the chair. "And the High Street shops will be closed afterward."

Sarah nodded as she took out a Voyage jumper of her own and held it up against herself. "So maybe tomorrow after school. Ugh, Vic, I wish I were going to the concert with you and not Max and the human ice sculpture." Sarah always referred to Max's fiancée, Lavinia, that way. She was so bloody frigid that Sarah sometimes wondered how Max kept his hands from freezing when he touched her. *Maybe he never does touch her*, Sarah thought with a grin. Max was such an honorable guy that Sarah figured he was waiting till he got married to even French kiss his fiancée. Max was a little too much of a straight arrow for her taste, but Sarah did love him to pieces. He was good to her, always had been. Especially since their mother died six years ago.

"Lavinia?" Victoria looked surprised. "Don't

tell me you still have to hang around with that beast. When does your punishment end? It's been, like, forever!"

"Tell me about it," Sarah muttered. Victoria was referring to Sarah's seemingly endless punishment for something she'd done a month ago. Something awful, really. But she hadn't meant her prank to go quite so awry. Here was what happened: She and Victoria had come up with a little trick to get Elizabeth fired, but for good reason. Elizabeth had been spying on Sarah at her father's request, and Sarah wasn't about to let that American geek follow her around and report on her misdeeds! So, Sarah had, um, sort of slashed Lavinia's wedding veil to bits and framed Elizabeth (quite well, if she did say so herself). And just moments before Elizabeth was being tossed out of Pennington House, Sarah had unfortunately chosen that very second to feel guilty . . . and her worried ruminations had been overheard by everyone! As punishment, Sarah had been grounded for two weeks, which had thankfully passed, and now she had to accompany Max and the ice princess on all sorts of outings and be ultranice to Elizabeth. If she tried to get out of one planned activity, Max would tell their father about the veil and framing incidents, and then Sarah would be really done for. Her father might even pull her out of school and hire her an all-day private tutor!

There was no worse punishment than having to be around the insufferable Lavinia and listen to her prattle endlessly about "what's expected of a lady in society." And Elizabeth? Well, Sarah had nothing against her, except maybe her annoyingly fresh-scrubbed look and polite, earnest, yes-ma'am ways. As for Max, Sarah truly did adore her brother. At least she got to spend some time with him. Even if she did have to endure the human ice sculpture.

"It's nice of them to take you to the concert," Victoria noted. "They sure are trying to make you happy. You'd think they'd be trying to torture you with the opera or a ballet or something horribly dull."

Sarah applied lip gloss and smacked her lips together. She did have to give her brother credit for caring and trying to bring her and Lavinia closer. But it would never happen. Lavinia would probably bring earplugs to the concert. And Max had probably had to bribe Icy into agreeing to go in the first place. Lavinia's favorite things to do were all deadly boring and very proper.

"At least you won't have to listen to wedding plans," Victoria said, joining Sarah by the mirror and trying the lip gloss herself. "The Bloody Young Blokes are way too loud for talk. They'll drown her out!"

Sarah laughed. Vic was absolutely right. And if she had to hear about that stupid wedding one more time, she'd scream! Ever since Lavinia and Max had announced their engagement, Lavinia had roped her into doing all sorts of wedding-related tasks. But now, with the wedding only a month away, things had calmed down a bit. Or at least, Lavinia was heaping errands on other people, like Niles Neesly, the fop of a wedding planner she'd hired.

"I can't wait to see Bones live onstage!" Sarah exclaimed as she whisked a bit of sparkly blush on her pale cheeks. "Maybe he'll even see me in the crowd and sing a song only to me." Sarah and Victoria dissolved in laughter. "Well, you never know."

A complete knowledge of the work of John Maynard Keynes is crucial in order to have a full understanding of . . .

Boooring! Who reads this tripe anyway? Max Pennington thought, slamming shut the book he'd been trying to wade through.

Who bloody cares about Keynsian economics? He pushed his dark hair out of his eyes and stared gloomily at the leather-bound tome in front of him. One hundred pages to read by Monday, and here it was, late Saturday afternoon, and he couldn't even get past the introduction. He pushed the book as far away from him as possible and leaned back in the deep leather wing chair that he'd ensconced himself in since arriving at the Bodleian Library half an hour before. He'd left his own extremely comfortable suite of rooms in the dorm in the hopes that the studious atmosphere of the library would motivate him to get some work done. But the fact that he'd read the same sentence over and over again without making any sense of it didn't bode well.

It's all such rot, he thought miserably. *I don't even want a degree in economics! Maybe I just won't finish my thesis. Then I won't get a degree in anything! Ha. Likely that I won't do what I'm supposed to. Story of my life.*

Max thought briefly about the fifty pages that he'd completed of his novel, a spy story. Now, *that* was something he could get into, but sons of earls didn't write spy novels. They went to Oxford and took useless degrees before taking their seat in Parliament, like their fathers and their fathers and their fathers. So Max, never one to make waves, had done as his father, grandfather, and countless generations of Penningtons before him and traipsed to Oxford to earn the expected degree. With honors of course.

Max couldn't help grinning as he imagined how his father would react if he told him that he didn't want to follow in his dull footsteps to Parliament, that he wanted to write this novel, become a journalist, maybe even a foreign correspondent in parts unknown.

And what about Lavinia, his picture-perfect fiancée; what would her reaction be if he asked her to read the first three chapters of his manuscript? Max pictured her in his mind's eye—so beautiful, so elegantly lovely, so perfect in every way that she made Princess Di look scruffy by comparison—and so cold, so boring that even reading about Keynsian economics was more fun than having a conversation with her.

Of course, there was *one* person who would want to read his novel.

Elizabeth.

Max closed his eyes briefly and allowed himself to think about Elizabeth. Something he'd been trying very hard *not* to do for the past month or so—ever since he'd shared that delicious kiss with her in the hallway.

Elizabeth. The lovely American who worked in the kitchen of his family home. She was so different from Lavinia. Where Lavinia went around in cashmere twinsets and custom-made Chanel trousers, Elizabeth wore the Pennington staff uniform—chinos and an oxford shirt. Where Lavinia was always perfectly coifed—her flaxen hair either in a French twist or in a golden tumble about her shoulders—Elizabeth sported a ponytail. And while Lavinia was ever conscious of her status as the duchess of Louster, Elizabeth was a kitchen maid.

Ha! Forget about the novel—what would my father say if he knew that I was besotted with one of our household staff? Max shook his head in dismay. If he hadn't fallen for Elizabeth so hard, he would have laughed at how clichéd the situation was—for centuries the nobility had been carrying on with the hired help.

But this isn't like that! Max protested silently. His feelings for Elizabeth went much deeper than the standard dalliance, and as for carrying on with her—well, except for that one kiss, they'd barely touched.

And I'll probably never kiss her again either! Max thought sadly. He'd been so shaken by their one brief embrace that he'd fled Pennington House and buried himself up at Oxford. He was quite literally afraid to spend too much time in her presence. Elizabeth was like a drug, one he was quickly becoming addicted to, and he couldn't afford that because in just a month, over Christmas weekend, he and Lavinia would wed.

Max wished that he could call the whole thing off. But he couldn't, because if going to Oxford was a Pennington tradition, marrying other members of the nobility was an unwritten *law*.

Max had known that he would marry Lavinia for a long time. He'd also known that his feelings for her didn't extend further than affection, but he hadn't really cared because he'd understood his duty. Both he and Lavinia were conscious that their union would merge their two families— each powerful in their own right—into a practically unstoppable force. The fact that his marriage was as much a business match as anything else had never bothered Max. Until now. Until Elizabeth.

"Got any reading done?"

James Leer, Max's best friend, sauntered over to the table where Max was sitting and flung his own economics text down on it.

"None," Max admitted ruefully, shifting his chair to make room for James. Although he knew he should get back to his work, he was glad for the interruption. James was the only person he could really talk to about what was going on. Partially because they'd been best friends practically since birth (James lived in the estate next door) and partially because James was in love with one of the Pennington House kitchen maids himself—Vanessa.

"Fancy a tandoori takeaway?" James asked as he settled himself in one of the deep leather chairs.

Max's mouth watered at the idea of having some Indian food, one of his favorites. "Absolutely. But I thought you had even more work to get through than I do."

"Yes, but I'm having about as much bloody luck." James sighed, his gray-blue eyes clouded over as he looked at Max.

"Let me guess—" Max laced his fingers behind his head. "Either you find the specifics of the Marshall Plan about as interesting as the newspaper that lined yesterday's basket of fish-and-chips, or you can't stop thinking about Vanessa. Possibly both."

"Spot on." James regarded Max shrewdly. "May I take it that this brilliant analysis means you're a fellow sufferer?"

"You know I am." Max groaned. He toyed with his Waterman pen for a second—a present from Lavinia—before tossing it aside and fixing his friend with a frank stare. "You know, James," he said after a brief pause. "To tell the truth, in some ways I can't help but envy you."

"Envy me?" James snorted in disbelief. "Of course, I admit that I'm by far the better-looking specimen, but"—he stretched his long legs out in front of him—"besides that, what else is there to envy?" He cocked an eyebrow at Max.

Max tore a sheet of paper out of his notebook and made a paper airplane, which he aimed at James's head.

James ducked and laughed. "Well, what, then?"

Max shrugged and started scribbling in his notebook. Like everything else he owned, it was expensive and beautiful. While other students at Oxford had standard spiral-bound notebooks, his were leather covered and emblazoned with the family crest, the paper inside a heavy parchment complete with watermark. He frowned at the crest for a moment before pushing the book away; it was a grim reminder of his position in life, a position that had already started to feel like a millstone around his neck rather than an honor and a privilege.

"You know what I'm talking about, James," Max said in all seriousness. "I know that things with Vanessa haven't gone exactly as you might have wished, but at least you're free to pursue her. You're not locked into a marriage that you don't want."

Although James came from a wealthy and powerful family, he wasn't the son of an earl with a thousand expectations heaped upon him. Sometimes, Max had to admit, he was *extremely* envious of James's situation.

"True," James said quietly, his gaze sympathetic. "But if it makes you feel any better, I'm just as unhappy as you are."

"I don't want you to be unhappy, James." Max shook his head. "God knows, I wouldn't wish the way I feel on anyone, let alone my best friend. I only mean that you're your own man. You don't have to follow along with some absurd family rules and regulations."

"Unfortunately, that hasn't helped me any with Vanessa." James sighed. "I've tried to forget about her, but nothing seems to help. Nothing, not burying myself in my work, not dating other girls, nothing." He leaned forward and put his elbows on the table. "Speaking of dating, did I mention that I have a date tonight?"

"No," Max said, surprised. "Anyone I know?"

"Allegra Templeton. She's studying classics over at Magdalen."

Max smiled. "She's a stunner."

"Maybe so, but she's not the stunner I want," James said moodily.

"Look, if you're not having any luck forgetting about Vanessa, maybe you should try pursuing her one last time," Max said reasonably.

"Come down to Pennington House tomorrow for brunch. Who knows what might happen?"

"Count me in," James said with a grin. "I'm surprised to hear you're risking a trip to the family homestead. I thought you were avoiding a certain blonde with blue-green eyes and an American accent. . . ."

Max nodded. He'd told James about the kiss and why he was avoiding Pennington House. "But I'm taking Lavinia and Sarah to a concert at the Palladium. We're going to see the Bloody Young Blokes."

"The Bloody Young Blokes?" James repeated, eyebrows raised. "I know they're superstars, but they're way too pop and way too teenage for my ears. Anyway, so if you're only picking up Sarah at the house, why will you be there for brunch tomorrow too?"

"The concert won't be over until well past midnight," Max explained. "By the time I drive Lavinia home and then Sarah home, I'll be too zonked to drive all the way back here." He spread his hands in a gesture of futility. "So, I'm planning to spend the night at the house."

"Well, don't look so sad about it," James commented. "Maybe seeing Elizabeth won't be so bad."

"Of course it won't be bad." Max sighed. The

main reason he was making excuses for sleeping at Pennington House was because he couldn't admit he wanted to see her. Needed to see her. He would simply have to keep his hands in his pockets to stop himself from grabbing her. A vision of Elizabeth's beautiful smiling face filled his head, and he imagined himself leaning in close to kiss her. What would happen if he tried to embrace her again? Would she respond as enthusiastically as she had the first time? What would happen if Lavinia caught him? Max took a deep breath. "Of course it won't be bad," he said, trying to blot out the bright shining vision of Elizabeth and focus his attention on James. "It'll be bloody fantastic to see her again. That's why I'm so worried!"

Chapter Two

"Do you go to Trinity?"

Eighteen-year-old Vanessa Shaw snapped up her head and stared at the guy sitting opposite her. She'd been staring gloomily out the train's window for the past ten minutes and hadn't even been aware that someone had sat down across from her.

Ever since Matilda had announced that the kitchen staff had the rest of the day off, she'd known exactly what she wanted to do. She wanted to take the train down to Oxford and confront James Leer. It had been a month since she'd seen him, and Vanessa was suspicious. He was keeping his distance for a reason. A reason she knew all too well. And it was making her too nervous. She had to get to the bottom of it.

Why hasn't he ratted on me? she wondered for

the thousandth time. She closed her eyes, remembering the shock on his face when he'd caught her snooping in the countess's private suite of rooms. Why hadn't he run straight to Max, or to the earl, or even simply to her boss, Mary, and reported that he'd found Vanessa, sans feather duster or vacuum, looking through the countess's desk? She clearly hadn't been in there to clean. Only Mary and her annoying little helper, Alice, were allowed in the countess's private sanctum to tidy up.

Vanessa wondered what James thought she'd been after. The family jewels? A stack of money? Any of the hideously expensive bibelots that Alice spent countless hours dusting? If James knew her the way he claimed to, he wouldn't believe her capable of theft. If he loved her the way he claimed to, he wouldn't think such a thing.

And since he was Max's best friend, he would never think the earl capable of anything awful. But the old man was capable of the worst things imaginable. And Vanessa was going to prove it. That was why she'd been searching through the countess's desk.

She was after proof. Proof that the earl of Pennington was her father.

After her mother's death last year, Vanessa had found a letter that her mother had written to the earl some nineteen years ago, a letter that made it clear that the esteemed earl was the father of her unborn child. Vanessa was sure that she hadn't misunderstood the contents of the letter—clearly her mother and the earl had been deeply in love. What she couldn't figure out was why her mother had been so resigned to the fact that the earl no longer wanted to have anything to do with her. *Mum should have been swanning around Pennington House instead of living in drunken squalor!* Vanessa shook her head angrily. The earl had had an affair with her mother, gotten her mother knocked up, then tossed her aside without a penny or a backward glance. Vanessa's mother had never recovered from the betrayal, and she'd lived her life a bitter drunk, going from boyfriend to boyfriend, living off the generosity of men. She'd died of alcohol poisoning, leaving behind a grieving daughter all alone in the world. A daughter who'd vowed never to end up like her mother.

Well, Mum may have given up, but that doesn't mean I have! Vanessa clenched her fists in determination. Once she'd discovered the letter among her mother's possessions, she hadn't wasted any time. She'd wormed her way into a job at Pennington House, intent on finding the evidence she needed to confront His Highness.

It had taken months to work up the nerve to approach his private study and his late wife's suite. And finally, Vanessa had found proof of their affair—a photo of the earl with her mother. But Vanessa had been startled by a noise and had hastily put the picture back, fearing she'd be caught. When she'd returned to collect the photo, it was gone. So, either the earl was aware that someone was snooping through his rooms, or Vanessa had simply forgotten which secret compartment she'd found it in. That seemed unlikely, though. Vanessa Shaw didn't forget anything. Anyway, she'd been searching like mad, only to be foiled again.

Sometimes Vanessa thought that the countess's private sanctum was as heavily guarded as the crown jewels. *And what happened when I was searching?* Vanessa thought bitterly. *James bloody Leer has to come and catch me!*

"I said, are you at Trinity?"

Vanessa shook herself slightly. She'd been totally lost in thought and forgot that the guy across from her had asked her a question.

"I . . . no." Vanessa wasn't sure whether to be flattered that she might look the part of a university girl or offended that he thought she looked like one of those upper-class brats who went to Oxford or Cambridge or wherever!

Of course if the earl hadn't deserted Mum, I probably would be studying at Oxford, Vanessa thought sadly.

"Well, what are you doing on the train to Oxford, then?" the guy asked flirtatiously.

Vanessa studied him from underneath her lashes. He was very fanciable, there was no doubt about that, but she was in no mood to flirt. Her mind was too busy trying to figure out just how she should approach James. She was feeling increasingly nervous as the train drew ever closer to the station, and her heart was beating against her ribs so loudly that she was surprised no one else could hear.

"I'm going to Oxford to meet someone," she said coldly, and returned to her magazine, but the words were a jumble in front of her eyes, and she could barely make sense of a single sentence.

I've got to get ahold of myself, she thought as she tossed the magazine aside. She took several deep breaths in an effort to calm down, but she couldn't stop her mind from racing through all the possible scenarios that awaited her at Oxford.

What if James refused to talk to her? What if he told her that he was planning on reporting her crime to the earl? What if he had *already* told, and they were just waiting to make their move? Catch her in the act again so that he could find out what she was looking for?

Vanessa leaned back against the plush of the seat. If James told her that her secret was safe, then the path was clear: She'd return to Pennington House and continue on her quest with renewed energy. Ever since he'd caught her, she'd been too afraid to search for the proof that she needed. But she'd had more than enough of skulking around the halls with a feather duster. It was time to put things into high gear; she couldn't wait to confront the earl. She couldn't wait to mete out the punishment that he so richly deserved.

But if James *had* told . . .

James holds my future in his hands, Vanessa thought, shuddering as the train drew into the station. *He holds my future in his hands, and I have to take it back.*

Sarah's palms stung from clapping so hard. *I can't believe that Max and the Ice Queen got such great tickets to the Bloody Young Blokes concert! Third row!* Sarah still couldn't quite get over her luck. Not only was the music so loud that Lavinia couldn't drone in her ear, but Bones McCall was even more gorgeous in the flesh than he had been on the page.

He has to be mine, Sarah decided absolutely as she watched him move across the stage. He was so sexy! So hot! So amazingly bloody cute!

Annoying thing was, every girl in England agreed with her. The concert hall on trendy

Wardour Street was packed to capacity with screaming girls.

As she scanned the throng of openmouthed fans, she saw several of her classmates. In fact, it looked like . . . *Is that Phillipa Ainsley front and center?* Sarah narrowed her eyes. The air was thick with smoke, and the lights in the club were dark, but she was sure that she saw Phillipa waving her hands to the beat and swaying back and forth as she fixed Bones with a predatory expression.

Back off! He's going to be mine! Sarah ordered telepathically, glaring at Phillipa before turning her attention back to Bones.

Mmmm, is he sexy! Sarah stared at him in fascination. She wondered what it would be like to kiss someone that hot. So far all the boys she'd kissed had been students at the Welles School, and *they* certainly couldn't compete with someone as absolutely fabulous as Bones McCall. Not even Nick, the last guy she'd fallen for.

Forget kissing Bones—what would it be like to have sex with him? Sarah bit her lip as she considered the idea. She'd come dangerously close to losing her virginity with Nick, who thank God had turned into an absolute toad before she'd lost her senses. She was glad she was still a virgin for someone as incredible as Bones. But she was definitely ready—sort of—for sex. At least she thought so.

Or maybe not. Argh! Who knew? So many people she knew were having sex—or claiming to anyway—and she wondered what she was missing. The thing sounded great, but more than a little scary. Would it hurt? What if the guy dumped her afterward for a virgin? What if the condom had a hole in it? She could get pregnant! Catch some horrible disease!

Sarah sighed. There was so much to think about when it came to sex and losing your virginity. Guys made it seem like it was all about "if you really cared about me . . . ," but it wasn't. That was only one piece of it. And frankly, how the hell did you know if the *guy* really cared about you!

Still, Bones was a worthy specimen. Worth thinking about it anyway.

Max leaned close and shouted in her ear, "Sarah, did I hear that Bones McCall is transferring to Welles?"

Sarah nodded excitedly. It was too loud to speak. She noticed Max lean back and casually drape an arm around Lavinia. She couldn't help wondering about the two of them. Were *they* having sex? She couldn't imagine the human ice sculpture doing anything that would actually muss her hair and makeup. Even now, in a smoke-filled room, surrounded by crowds, Lavinia looked like she had stepped out of *Vogue* magazine.

Oh, who cares what they do? Sarah shrugged and turned back to watch Bones. She didn't want to spend too much time wondering about whether Lavinia was a virgin, which she was sure she was. Sarah had much better things to worry about. As she watched Bones sway his hips on the stage, a much more interesting question presented itself.

Was she finally ready to lose *her* virginity?

"Hmmm, this wine is absolutely lovely, James," Allegra Templeton said, tipping her glass and draining the last of the exclusive vintage that James had poured for them both. "It's just what I needed too. I've been toiling away for the past few hours on a perfectly vile essay." She smiled at him from where she sat, cross-legged on his bed in his suite at the university.

James nodded. "I know how that goes." He thought of his own failed attempts to work on his thesis. The subject matter fascinated him; that wasn't the problem. And he was quite studious and focused. The problem was one dark-haired, brown-eyed creature named Vanessa Shaw.

James leaned back in his desk chair and laced his hands behind his head as he looked at Allegra. Max had been right—she *was* a stunner. Her tight, pale pink sweater and sexy jeans made the most of her slim, curvaceous figure. And he did like her long, red hair. More, she was sitting on his *bed*, for God's sake! Still, James couldn't bring himself to be any more interested in her than he was in working on his thesis. All he could think about was Vanessa and the questions swirling in his mind. Such as what the hell she'd been doing in the countess's suite, snooping around the desk. Such as what she'd been looking for. She'd looked horrified enough when he'd caught her that he'd known she'd been up to no good. But what?

There was no way Vanessa, his Vanessa, was a thief. He would never believe that. Granted, he didn't know her that well, hadn't even had a very long conversation with her. But he'd watched her very closely in the many months she'd been working at Max's house. Listened to her bits of conversation with the other maids, watched her eyes take in everything. Oh, those gorgeous brown eyes! That beautiful heart-shaped face that seemed so vulnerable!

He realized he was being rude to Allegra. He was hardly even keeping up his end of the conversation. He took a deep breath and forced himself to come up with something to say. "I can't seem to get any work done lately," he managed, giving his date a small smile.

"Really?" Allegra arched her perfect eyebrows. "What seems to be the problem?"

James shrugged. He knew what the problem was—*he* was obsessed with Vanessa Shaw and *she* couldn't be bothered to give him the time of day—but he could hardly discuss that with Allegra. More, ever since he'd caught her red-handed in the countess's suite, he'd avoided her. She wouldn't tell him what she'd been doing; he'd asked for the truth that night he'd come upon her, asked her to trust him. But she wouldn't tell him anything. And there was no way he'd report finding her snooping to the Penningtons. So he'd had no choice but to just disappear. To just give up and disappear. Vanessa apparently had her demons, and whatever she was doing, she didn't want him involved . . . or involved in her life.

"More wine?" he asked Allegra.

"Super," Allegra murmured, uncrossing her long, shapely legs and leaning forward to give James her glass.

James couldn't help noticing her legs, but nothing would ever take his mind off Vanessa.

He sighed inwardly as he topped off her glass. James wished that he was attracted to Allegra. Any man in his right mind would be—she was extremely attractive, intelligent, and witty. The only problem was, she wasn't Vanessa.

Why am I so enthralled by that girl? he wondered as he smiled at Allegra. *She's got one of the*

sharpest tongues I've ever heard and a terrible tem-
per; she's made it clear that she doesn't have very
good feelings for me; she's doing who knows what in
the countess's suite. James's brow furrowed. *And*
yet I'm hopelessly smitten.

"James, are you listening? You look about a
million miles away." Allegra frowned slightly.

"Sorry." James waved his hand in a dismissive
gesture. "I was just—" He was interrupted mid-
sentence by a knock at the door.

"Expecting someone?" Allegra asked. She
looked somewhat irritated.

"No." James got up from his chair. "Of course,
Marcus from down the hall often borrows my
textbooks. . . ." He flung open the door, expecting to see the burly rugby player who had the next
room down.

But it wasn't Marcus who was waiting outside.
Instead James found himself staring into the mysterious brown eyes of Vanessa Shaw. He'd spent so
much time daydreaming about her the last few
weeks that he wasn't completely sure that he
wasn't dreaming now.

"Well, aren't you going to ask me in?" Vanessa
asked sharply.

"Vanessa . . . I . . ." James was at a loss for
words. Having her show up at his room unan-
nounced was better than anything he could ever

have dreamed, but why did she have to come when he was on a date with another girl?

"Who's there, James?" Allegra got up from the bed and wandered over.

Vanessa's eyes widened, and she stepped back, clearly startled. "I see you have company," she said quickly as her eyes flickered past him and took in Allegra. "Sorry," she said, her cheeks reddening before she turned and fled down the hall.

"I—I . . . ," James stammered. "Vanessa!" he called after her. He half started out the door and then paused. Could he really run after her and just leave Allegra?

"James, who was that?" Allegra asked, her voice frosty.

"Um—" James dropped down in his desk chair. He was speechless.

"Perhaps it's time I was going as well," Allegra announced angrily as she struggled into her coat.

"I'm sorry, Allegra," James said quietly as she brushed past him. He knew that he should offer to walk her home, but he couldn't bring himself to. His mind was too filled with images of Vanessa. She'd looked positively stricken when she'd spotted him with another woman. Did that mean that she had feelings for him? That she could possibly care for him more than she was willing to let on?

She must have some feelings for me, or she wouldn't have come all the way out here, James told himself. Then again, Vanessa was hard to read. Maybe she wasn't there because she cared for him. Maybe she'd finally decided to tell him her secret about what she'd been doing in the countess's suite. *But why now after an entire month?* James wondered.

He really had no idea what was on Vanessa's mind. One thing was for certain, though: He was determined to find out what her big secret was. And whether she liked it or not, he was going to Pennington House tomorrow to find out.

At first I was just angry at everyone, but now I'm starting to miss them too. Sometimes something will happen that I want to tell Jessica about, and then I remember that I'm thousands of miles away, and that I haven't spoken to her in months, and, um, oh, yeah, I vowed never to forgive her or speak to her again! At times I feel so lonely that I want to get back in touch—to forgive—and at other times I just don't know. . . .

Elizabeth threw down her pen. It seemed to her that she'd been writing the same self-pitying drivel in her journal for months now. She was getting bored of voicing the same tired old complaints. Yeah, she had no one to talk to, but after all, she was the one who'd decided to cut herself off from her family and friends. Of course she'd had more than enough provocation, but still . . .

She got up from where she was sitting cross-legged on the bed and wandered restlessly around the small attic room that she shared with Vanessa and Alice, both of whom were out for the night. In fact, the rest of the staff, not to mention the Penningtons themselves, were out. Elizabeth had the entire house to herself.

But that just makes me feel even lonelier, she thought as she paced back and forth. *I should be glad that I'm alone for a change. After all, the way Matilda and Mary run me ragged, I never get a moment to myself.*

Elizabeth sighed as she flopped back down on the bed again. *Maybe I'd be happier if I didn't keep torturing myself by thinking about Max!* Elizabeth had been hoping that when he arrived to pick up Sarah, he'd take a moment to say hello to her. *After all, we did kiss the last time he was here,* she reminded herself wistfully. But Max had dashed into the house and dashed back out with Sarah in tow barely two minutes later.

What did you expect? She punched the pillow in frustration. *That he'd run up here and declare his undying love?*

Well, I had kinda hoped . . .

Elizabeth knew she was being ridiculous. Max had already told her that his obligations toward his family outweighed his feelings for her. How much more explicit did he have to be before it sank into her thick head?

She jumped off the bed. She'd had enough of hanging around the gloomy room with only her thoughts for company. *Even Alice has a date tonight!* Elizabeth thought as she headed down the stairs toward the kitchen. The meek housekeeper's assistant was sweet but could barely look at someone of the opposite sex, let alone speak to them. And Vanessa had left long ago for who knew where and who knew what.

And here I am, brooding over Max and raiding the refrigerator, Elizabeth mused miserably as she swung open the refrigerator and peered inside. There was enough food to feed an army for at least a week. Of course there had to be. The staff had to be prepared for any and every desire that the family might have. Who knew when Sarah would call down for an order of fat-free scones or the earl would require a little pickled herring?

And of course there's Max and his midnight Häagen-Dazs fix, Elizabeth thought, remembering how she'd first met him. He'd literally bumped into her on the stairs on his way to the kitchen for a bowl of cherry-chocolate ice cream.

46

The tension had shimmered between them even then. *I think I fell for him right away!* Elizabeth spooned some ice cream into one of the exquisite Sevres dishes that served as the "casual" china and sat down at the table.

The sound of a car pulling up outside made Elizabeth start. Max! Of course it *could* be the earl, but it sounded more like Max's Jaguar.

Elizabeth slipped soundlessly to the window by the door. She pulled the lace curtain aside and peeked out. Sure enough, the Jaguar was there, and Sarah was climbing out of the back.

Elizabeth tensed, waiting for a glimpse of Max, but he didn't seem to be getting out of the car. *Of course, he has to take Lavinia home,* Elizabeth realized. As she watched, Lavinia leaned in toward Max and kissed him deeply.

Whoa! Smoking! Elizabeth gasped. What happened to the ice-princess act? She was surprised that the windows hadn't fogged over. An image of the chaste kiss that she and Max had shared flashed in front of her eyes, and she blushed in embarrassment. No wonder he'd had such an easy time avoiding her. What had seemed like a passionate embrace to her was probably about as exciting as a game of jacks to Max. She took one last look at the couple in the car, tears of anger and longing welling up in her eyes.

47

So, Elizabeth thought, letting the curtain fall back into place. *I guess that's what duty and obligation look like.*

Except it doesn't look like duty and obligation, Elizabeth knew as she rinsed out her empty dish. *It looks like they're hot and heavy into each other!*

She could understand why the realization hurt her so badly. She'd wanted so much to believe Max when he'd told her that he wasn't in love with Lavinia, but she couldn't figure out why she was so surprised. Even if Lavinia wasn't the love of his life, why *wouldn't* they be sleeping together? After all, they were engaged to be married.

Except I thought that Max was a virgin, like me. I thought that we . . . Elizabeth couldn't bring herself to finish the thought. She knew that she had to stop fantasizing about Max. Nothing would come of it except her own heartbreak.

I guess I won't be kissing him again.

Face it, Elizabeth thought. *I was the last virgin in America, and I'll be the last virgin in England!*

"Lavinia!"

Max gasped as he came up for air. *What's gotten into you?* he couldn't help adding silently. Lavinia wasn't usually given to such outbursts of affection. In fact, Max didn't remember her *ever* kissing him like that. Not even when he'd proposed to her.

48

"Yes?" She arched an eyebrow at him. As always, she looked coolly beautiful, especially now, with the moonlight streaming through the windows and backlighting her glorious golden hair.

Max knew that most guys would kill to have a girl like Lavinia pounce on them the way she just had. He shook his head as he put the car into reverse. *So why do I have to keep thinking of Elizabeth?*

"The concert was fun, wasn't it?" he asked in a light tone as he drove away from Pennington House. "Sarah had a blast." *I just wish that my sister would warm up to you,* he thought, glancing at Lavinia. *But I guess I can hardly blame her. After all, we're about to get married, and I haven't warmed up to you!*

"It's such a beautiful night," Lavinia said. "Maybe we shouldn't rush home just yet."

Max looked across at her in surprise. Lavinia wasn't one to behave spontaneously; in fact, it was as out of character as that passionate embrace had been. Not only that, but he knew she'd planned to get up early to buy some last-minute items for her trousseau, and it was already well past midnight. Why would she want to stay up even later?

"Really, Max," Lavinia added, turning toward him. Her alabaster skin looked even more luminous in the light that streamed in through the car windows. "Why don't we drive down to Epping Forest and look at the stars?"

"But Lavinia," Max protested as they sped to-ward London. "That's miles away!"

"So?" Lavinia asked. She shifted in her seat so that she could lean against Max. "I think it would be romantic, don't you?" She traced the curve of his biceps with her long, elegant fingers and feath-ered kisses down along his jaw.

Max was so surprised that he nearly swerved off the road. He couldn't remember Lavinia ever be-having this way before.

"I—I don't know what to say," Max stammered.

"Don't say anything, Max," Lavinia murmured in a seductive voice as they drew up outside the es-tate where she lived with her aunt and uncle. "Let's leave the talking aside."

Lavinia pressed her lips against his and slid her arms around his neck.

What's wrong with me? Max thought, cursing himself inwardly as he felt Lavinia's slim curves mold themselves to his chest. Unfortunately Max knew all too well what was wrong with him. He couldn't stop thinking about Elizabeth. As Lavinia kissed him even deeper, a vision of Elizabeth's sweet face flashed in front of him. He disengaged her hands and pulled away from Lavinia as gently as he could.

"What's the matter?" Lavinia asked, looking a bit stung. "My aunt and uncle are away for the weekend."

"I'm sorry, Lavinia," Max said, "but, uh, I'm so behind on my thesis, and I'd planned to burn the midnight oil tonight. . . ."

"Oh," Lavinia said, clearly appeased. "Well, you do need to get the thesis done. Honestly, Max, you should have been done months ago. The way you procrastinate, I swear, you're like a child! But—" She traced a finger seductively down his cheek. "That doesn't mean you can't come in for just a little while. . . ."

Max stared at Lavinia openmouthed. What had happened to the girl who'd insisted that she remain a virgin until their wedding night? What happened to the usual dry peck on the lips?

Lavinia must suspect, Max thought grimly. Of course! He was an idiot not to have seen it before. Lavinia was no fool; she must sense that he was gradually becoming more detached, that his feelings were drifting elsewhere. . . . This must be her way of enticing him back. Unfortunately, it wasn't working.

Max's lack of a response seemed response enough for Lavinia. "Well, if your thesis is more important than your future bride, far be it from me to keep you from it," she snapped as she flung open the car door. "I'll expect a call from you tomorrow; that is, if you can bear to tear yourself away from your work." She jumped out of the car and walked swiftly up the drive.

What have I done? Max groaned as he watched her departing back. He knew that he should go after her, but he couldn't bring himself to. He also knew that things couldn't go on the way they had. He cared about Lavinia, but he cared deeply about Elizabeth. It was unthinkable that he call off the wedding, but it was also unthinkable that he could stop himself from dreaming day and night about Elizabeth.

With a deep sigh Max reversed out of the drive and headed back toward Pennington House. Whatever happened, he had a bad feeling that someone was going to get hurt.

Chapter
Three

"More polish, Vanessa! And more muscle!" Mary ordered as she strode into the dining room.

Vanessa frowned as she drew a finger down the length of the Georgian rosewood table she was polishing for today's stupid brunch. Did Mary want the food to slide off the bloody table?

Mary's eagle eyes roved every inch of the table. "Still some dust! When I come back, I'd better see my reflection in the wood."

Well, I wouldn't want you to scare yourself, Vanessa thought, fighting the urge to laugh in Mary's face. *As if I could laugh. There's nothing funny about my life. Nothing!*

Why am I in such a bad bloody mood? Vanessa asked herself as Mary trotted off. Vanessa rubbed the table to a brilliant shine. *I don't even like James, so what do I care if he's with some toffee-voiced prig who uses too much eyeliner?*

Vanessa stopped polishing the table and stretched the kinks out of her back with a sigh. She'd barely slept since bursting in on James and his girlfriend or whoever she was. Vanessa had been too keyed up—anxiety over whether or not he'd reported her to Max or the earl had vied with shock over seeing him with that girl.

I've got to stop thinking about James! Vanessa chided herself as she placed an ornate silver candelabra in the center of the table. She knew that she had to focus on her mission. She needed to find that photo or other proof that the earl was her father, *not* worry about who James's nocturnal companions were. That way she could confront the earl, destroy his happy little home, shove the truth of the great earl of Pennington in his children's snot-nosed faces, and then finally quit this crummy job and take off.

But what will James think when I destroy the earl and his family? Vanessa couldn't help asking herself. She pushed the delicate white oak chairs back against the table and picked up her dust cloth and the can of polish

"Vanessa," Matilda said, poking her head around the door. "Do you think you could go to the herbarium and get me some more rosemary?

I'm afraid I don't have enough." She handed Vanessa a pair of pruning shears and the small basket that they always used for gathering herbs.

Vanessa sighed and took the basket, swinging it in a wide arc as she walked through the French doors that led from the dining room to the garden. She was tired of worrying. As soon as she was done with the after-brunch cleanup, she'd take a brief nap and then start on her hunt for evidence. She wasn't going to think about . . .

James! Vanessa gasped at the sight of his car parked next to Max's Jaguar. What was he doing at Pennington House? Had he come to confront her? Was he so angry at her bursting in on his little love scene last night that he'd finally decided to have his revenge? Vanessa turned cold as she considered the possibilities.

Maybe he just wants to have breakfast with his buddy, Vanessa tried to reassure herself. James often came over for meals with the Penningtons.

What was going to happen? She hoped that Mary would have Elizabeth serve and keep Vanessa in the kitchen because she didn't fancy coming face-to-face with James over the kippers and eggs.

Maybe I should just go back to bed, Vanessa thought as an enormous yawn nearly split her face in two. There was almost nothing that she would rather have done at that moment than turn tail and head upstairs, but she knew that was impossible. *I'd lose my job in a flash if I did that.*

"Vanessa?" Elizabeth called to her across the lawn from the kitchen. "Matilda says to hurry up with the rosemary. Do you need any help?"

I need a lot of help. Vanessa smirked as she picked up the pace. *But not with the bleeding rosemary!*

Even the hustle and bustle of the morning rush as the staff raced to prepare brunch wasn't enough to take Elizabeth's mind off the image of Max and Lavinia kissing.

"Here's the rosemary," Vanessa said, coming into the kitchen with the herb basket over her arm. She carelessly tossed a few sprigs of the fragrant herb down on the cutting board.

"Thanks," Elizabeth said, giving Vanessa a sidelong glance. *She looks about as good as I feel. Maybe her night wasn't any better than mine.*

"Hurry up with that vegetable chopping, Elizabeth," Mary said as she came in with several bunches of flowers from the greenhouse. "The earl will be down any minute now, and you know that it won't do to keep him waiting." She began arranging the flowers into small bouquets and placing them into individual silver bud vases.

I'm hurrying, I'm hurrying, Elizabeth grumbled

inwardly. She wasn't in the best of moods, and Mary's scolding didn't make her feel any better.

"And for goodness' sake, chop that shallot finer!" Mary continued as she whisked out of the room with the vases.

Yeah, yeah, Elizabeth muttered to herself. Mary could be incredibly bossy at times, and after five months of working at Pennington, Elizabeth was rarely affected by Mary's moodiness. But the woman was getting on her nerves this morning.

She grabbed the rosemary and began shredding it into a fine chiffonade. *I wonder if he even bothered to come home last night.*

"Hurry up with those herbs, Elizabeth," Matilda said as she broke half a dozen eggs into a bowl and added a generous dash of cream. "I needed them five minutes ago."

I'm going as fast as I can, Elizabeth silently yelled.

The kitchen door swung open, and Elizabeth glanced up. Max.

Their eyes locked, and it was as if they were alone in the room. Elizabeth stared at him; he was even more handsome than she remembered. Tall, dark, and hot. *And not interested in you,* she reminded herself, *kiss or no kiss. That kiss meant zippo to Max. Not when he's getting much hotter stuff from his very own fiancée!*

57

It was hard to tell what Max was thinking. He looked away from Elizabeth and spoke to Matilda.

"Matilda, we'll be one extra for breakfast—James is here as well. Sorry I didn't let you know before, but I didn't get in until very late last night."

I'll just bet you didn't, Elizabeth thought savagely as she hacked at the rosemary.

"All right, Max," Matilda said agreeably. "Elizabeth, hurry up, will you? I need that rosemary double-quick now."

Aargh! Elizabeth hacked at the rosemary. She chopped as fast as she could, but the knife was rather slippery, and she missed the rosemary and hit her thumb instead.

"Ouch!" she cried. She dropped the knife and examined her hand. The cut seemed rather deep, and she winced in pain.

Max was at her side in an instant. He tenderly took her hand and examined the cut. "This looks rather deep," he said. "I think I should take you to a doctor."

"Don't be silly," Elizabeth managed to choke out. "It's barely more than a scratch." The cut stung, but it was well worth it to see the depth of Max's concern for her. *He does care,* she told herself as his dark head bent over her hand. *He does, or he wouldn't be acting like this.*

"Well, maybe you don't need a Harley Street

specialist," Max said. "But you'll at least let me bandage this for you."

"I hardly think you need bother yourself with that." Mary bustled over. "I can take care of things well enough. Let me see that, Elizabeth." She planted herself between the two of them. "I think I can handle this," she continued, briskly efficient as she reached into her apron pocket and came out with a Band-Aid. "A little bit of sticking plaster is all you need," Mary insisted, deftly bandaging the cut while Max looked over her shoulder at Elizabeth.

She's right—that's all my hand needs, Elizabeth thought as she returned to the rosemary. *But what about my heart?*

"Wonderful as always, Matilda," James said politely as he took a large bite of his omelette.

"It's always a pleasure to cook for you," Matilda said, beaming at James before whisking back into the kitchen with an empty platter.

James took another bite of his omelette. It *was* delicious, but it might have been made out of sawdust for all he cared. He was much too nervous to notice what he ate. He'd arrived at Pennington House half an hour earlier, desperate to see Vanessa, but so far only Elizabeth and Alice had presented themselves at the table.

59

Where is she? he wondered as he broke open a freshly baked roll and spread it with marmalade. *And more important, why did she come to see me last night?*

As much as he wanted to believe that she'd simply gone all the way to Oxford with the idea of seeing him, James knew that was hardly likely. After all, she'd repulsed all of his advances before. What would have made her change her mind suddenly?

Elizabeth came into the room with a plate of kippers for the earl. James smiled sympathetically as he took in the expression on Max's face. He looked totally besotted. *I'm sure that's what I look like whenever Vanessa's around. . . .*

Vanessa! James nearly dropped his fork as Vanessa walked in, carrying a heavy teapot. She struggled a little, trying to balance the creamer and sugar that were next to it on the tray that she held, and it was all James could do not to leap up and help her.

He could see that the earl was staring at him and hastily shifted his gaze back to his eggs.

"So James," the earl began, folding his paper in half and holding out his cup for a refill. "I do hope that your thesis is progressing somewhat faster than Max's. Whenever I ask him about it, he positively cringes."

"Actually, I'm really not doing all that much

better," James said. He watched Vanessa out of the corner of his eye as she poured for the earl. *She's so beautiful,* he thought. Her porcelain skin glowed in the soft morning light, and her movements were graceful as she moved from the earl to Max with the teapot.

James quickly swallowed his nearly full cup so that he could ask for a refill. "Uh, actually I'd like a little more," he said as Vanessa headed back toward the door. She spun around and glared at James.

James held out his cup. She was so close as she poured that he could smell her perfume, a light flowery scent that made him want to grab her. Her wrist brushed his as she straightened up, and James caught her gaze for a moment. Their eyes locked, and he couldn't help feeling that she'd just as soon pour the tea over his head as she would into his cup.

Why is she so angry with me? James shook his head in bewilderment. She must know that he'd kept her secret about finding her in the countess's suite.

Could she have been stealing? James briefly wondered with a frown. He couldn't imagine anyone as fiercely proud as Vanessa stooping to pilfer some silver fountain pens. But what other explanation could there be? He hated to think that she was a thief, but if she had been up to something iffy, he was sure that she had an excellent reason for it. *If only she'd trust me,* he thought for the thousandth time.

"Well, if you two fellows will excuse me," the earl said, "I've got quite a lot of work to do." He gave Max a stern look. "You might want to follow my example and sit down with your thesis for a change."

Max nodded, but as soon as the earl was out of the dining room, he turned to James with a quizzical look and whispered, "Am I wrong, or is there even more tension between you and Vanessa this morning?"

"I'm afraid you're right," James said, crumpling his napkin. "Vanessa came to my room at Oxford last night while Allegra was there."

"Phew," Max whistled.

"I'm going to see if I can find her," James said, standing up. "It's time we had things out between us."

Max nodded. "Good luck."

I need it, James thought grimly as he left the dining room. *Now, where would Vanessa be?* He looked up and down the hall. He hoped she wasn't in the kitchen—he had no desire to carry out a conversation under the prying eyes of Matilda and the rest of the kitchen staff.

A flash of dark hair caught his eye. *There she is!* He walked over to the French doors that led outside. She was walking toward the herbarium with a pair of pruning shears in her hand and a basket under her arm.

James quickly stepped through the doors and

out into the cool November morning. "Vanessa," he called.

Vanessa whirled around. "Why are you following me?"

"I only want to talk to you," James said, taking a tentative step forward.

"Well, I'm not interested in talking to you," Vanessa flared angrily. She turned on her heel and stalked off toward the herbarium.

"Vanessa! Wait." James sprinted after her into the herbarium. "I need to talk to you."

The air was warm, and James was overpowered for a second by the heavy fragrance that filled the glass walls.

What a romantic setting, he couldn't help thinking. Why couldn't he just take Vanessa in his arms? Why did they have to be adversaries?

"I can't imagine what you have to say to me," Vanessa snapped angrily as she began cutting some sprigs of thyme. "If you need someone to talk to, why don't you look up that girl who was in your room last night?"

James couldn't help grinning. So Vanessa was jealous. "I want to talk to you," he said as he drew closer. "Not to Allegra."

"Well, go ahead—I don't seem to be able to stop you," Vanessa said, not looking at James as she snipped away at the herbs.

"I want you to feel like you can trust me," James said quietly. "I want you to know that your secrets will be safe with me."

"Will they?" Vanessa whirled around and fixed him with a steely glare. "How am I to know that? Why should I trust you?"

James took a step closer. He longed to hold her. In spite of her angry tone and defiant stance, he could see that she was frightened. "Why can't you see that I'm a friend? I haven't told anyone about what I saw. Doesn't that make you trust me even a little?" He thought he saw tears shimmering in her eyes, but her face was lowered, and it was impossible to tell. "Won't you tell me what's going on?" he persisted gently. "I want to help. . . ." James put his hand under Vanessa's chin and raised her head so that she could see into his eyes.

Vanessa was silent for a moment, and James was thrilled at the electricity that shimmered between them.

But the moment was shattered when she twisted away with a look of fury. "Leave me alone!" she cried. She raced out of the herbarium.

If only I could, he thought sadly.

Chapter Four

"You look absolutely stunning, my bride," Max said as he looked deep into Elizabeth's eyes.

"As do you, husband to be," Elizabeth whispered. She'd never felt so beautiful, so special, so cherished in her whole life.

"Let me fix your veil," Jessica Wakefield offered. Elizabeth's sister fiddled with the yards of Belgian lace until they framed her face perfectly. "You look like a princess," Jessica said, smiling proudly.

"So do you," Elizabeth said. Jessica did look like a princess in her pink silk dress. The other brides-maids were wearing varying shades of peach.

Alice Wakefield, Elizabeth's mother, also looked beautiful in her dress. "Now, Ned, the wedding hasn't started yet; you're not allowed to cry now," she gently admonished her husband, who was discreetly wiping his eyes.

"The same goes for you, Dad," Max told the earl.

"I can't believe my little girl is going to be known as Lady Elizabeth," Elizabeth's mom said.

Elizabeth smiled. She didn't know if that was true; the English titles system was so confusing! But she sure liked the sound of it! Lady Elizabeth. Elizabeth clutched her bouquet; the fragrant lilacs and lush peonies were as beautiful as an impressionist painting. She turned to glance at the tables set up underneath the gaily striped yellow-and-green tents, where dozens of waiters were scurrying about, laying out platters and silver bowls. Elizabeth turned back to Max, and they shared a secret smile—they were both thinking the same thing— that if things hadn't worked out so perfectly, Elizabeth would have been the one serving the caviar, and Lavinia would have been carrying the peonies.

Thank God Lavinia decided to join a convent a week before she and Max were supposed to be married!

"What's that buzzing?" Elizabeth wondered as an unpleasant ringing intruded. *Ugh,* she thought, realizing she'd been dreaming. *As if such a thing could possibly happen.*

"Would you turn off that bleeding alarm clock?" Vanessa's voice pierced the air.

"Yeah, yeah, good morning to you too." Elizabeth's arm shot out from underneath the covers, and she shut off the alarm. *Well, it was nice while it lasted,* she thought with a small smile as she went over some of the details of her dream. *But I don't know that I'd be into caviar, and besides, Jessica would look better in blue. . . .*

Jessica. Elizabeth sat up as the full meaning of her dream hit home. Of course there was nothing so amazing about her dreaming that she and Max were about to be married. Hadn't she studied Freud in freshman psych? It was called wish fulfillment, she remembered as she jumped out of bed and headed for the bathroom. But what did it mean that her family was in the dream?

She'd certainly dreamed about them plenty of times in the last five months, but *those* dreams had been nightmares. Elizabeth shuddered as she recalled images of Jessica turning into a snake and hissing at her. What did it mean that she was having *pleasant* dreams about them?

Am I finally able to forgive Jessica and my parents? Elizabeth asked herself as she took a quick shower, put her hair into its usual ponytail, and hurried unto her uniform.

She considered the proposition seriously as she, Vanessa, and Alice went downstairs and into the kitchen for their breakfast. *No,* she thought, shaking her head as she helped herself to some tea. *I'm not ready to forgive them yet; I'm just seriously missing them. I don't know why, but it seems to be getting worse lately.*

The kitchen staff ate in silence and then prepared breakfast for the Penningtons in silence. Everyone seemed in her own world. Finally Matilda broke the quiet. "Take the bacon into the dining room," she said, handing Elizabeth a huge silver platter of sizzling bacon.

Elizabeth took the tray and headed out into the dining room. The earl and Max were already down there, but Sarah was nowhere to be seen. Elizabeth could barely drag her eyes away from Max. He looked particularly good this morning . . . *almost as handsome as he did in my dream.*

Max glanced at her over the rim of his teacup and gave her a small answering smile.

It's like he can read my thoughts. Elizabeth's heart beat faster, and she nearly dropped the platter.

"Let me help you with that," Max said, instantly at her side. He took the heavy platter and placed it on the table. "Is your hand better?" he asked, a concerned expression on his face.

"Oh, yes, I'd already forgotten about it," Elizabeth replied, glancing at the Band-Aid on her thumb.

"I'm sure that Elizabeth is quite capable of serving the meal by herself," the earl boomed. It was clear that he wasn't pleased by Max's concern.

"Of course, I—I . . ." Elizabeth blushed and stammered, but the earl ignored her and focused his attention on Max.

"By the way, Max, isn't Niles Neesly coming round today?" he asked, referring to the hideously expensive wedding planner that Lavinia had insisted on.

"Uh, no, actually he's coming on Wednesday." Max avoided Elizabeth's eyes as he answered.

Oh, who am I kidding? Elizabeth asked herself as she scooped up an empty platter and returned to the kitchen. Maybe Max liked her enough to bandage her hand, but he obviously had his mind on other things. *Let's face it,* Elizabeth thought as she banged the platter down and grabbed her half-empty cup of tea, which was now stone-cold. *I'm not going to make up with my family, and I'm not going to marry Max either!*

A sewer would smell ambrosial compared to this! Vanessa shuddered. She pressed a handkerchief to her nose and tried to ignore the mingled odors of overcooked cabbage and stale laundry that wafted through the air as she climbed the rickety stairs to the flat she used to live in with her mother.

She didn't even know why she'd come. Perhaps just to remind herself what the earl's cruelty had done to her mum.

Vanessa sighed deeply as she raised her hand to touch the graffiti-scarred door. She was suddenly reminded of the last time she saw her mother. Her mum had been living with a boyfriend, Colin, and was sick. Colin had called the number Vanessa had given him for emergencies, and Vanessa had known something was terribly wrong the minute she'd heard Colin's voice.

Vanessa remembered blinking back tears of frustration and sadness as she'd walked into her mother's flat and seen her lying on her bed. Her mother had looked even paler than usual, her once beautiful hair was matted and filthy, and her lips, which she was licking feverishly in her sleep, were parched and flaking. Vanessa had sat on the side of the bed and stroked her mother's forehead, which had felt too warm. Colin had been right to call. Vanessa could remember feeling grateful that at least her mum had a man who cared about her.

And then anger had overtaken her. Her mother should have been comfortably ensconced in the countess's elegant suite of rooms instead of this filthy hole. The earl should have been sitting by her side, barking orders at the servants while a Harley Street specialist attended to her.

This is the earl's fault! Vanessa clenched her fists as she thought of how comfortable and happy his life was compared to how her mum's had been. Compared to anyone's, for that matter. He'd probably never known a moment of misery, while her mother had spent the last twenty years in poverty. *He's responsible for my mother's sorry life and death! He used her for his pleasure and then discarded her like so much rubbish!*

Vanessa took a deep breath. She had to learn to control her rage. It was so easy to let it consume her, and that was a luxury she couldn't afford. Instead she had to use her anger, she had to let it fuel her quest so she could find the proof she needed and destroy the earl and his family like he had destroyed hers.

It's a good thing I came here after all, Vanessa thought grimly. She needed to remember, to be reminded of just how terrible her mother's life had been. How terrible *her* own life had been because of it. Her focus had been drifting lately. She'd allowed herself to spend entirely too much time thinking about James. How could she possibly have been fool enough to have found his attentions flattering? Wealthy, privileged guys always had an eye for a pretty girl. They were all like the earl, and Vanessa shuddered at how she'd reacted to finding James with another woman.

Amazing to think that she'd been affected by it at all. Who cared? If anything, she'd been saved. *I shan't waste any more energy thinking about James Leer. I'm just bloody grateful that he's been so tied up with someone else that he hasn't had the time to reveal my secret.*

"Um, scrumptious, but I already have at least three black cashmere jumpers," Sarah said as she took the cropped turtleneck from Victoria and held it up against herself. She gazed at her reflection in the full-length mirror in Warehouse, one of her favorite boutiques.

Both girls had cut history to go shopping on High Street, but so far they hadn't come up with anything that Sarah had liked or at least anything that she thought would catch Bones McCall's eye.

There's no telling when he'll even show up at school, Sarah thought as she rifled through the racks of dresses that hung on the opposite wall. So far neither Bones McCall *nor* Phillipa Ainsley had shown their faces at Welles, but Sarah wasn't taking any chances—she wanted to be prepared when Bones showed up. Of course, she had to wear her uniform at school, but *after* school . . . she was sure that Bones would frequent the local hot spots, and she intended to be there, in the most fetching ensemble that she could find. *This looks like a possibility,* she thought, pulling out a slinky pale blue matte jersey dress.

"Too tarty by half," Victoria said.

"Hmmm." Sarah held the dress at arm's length and studied it critically. "You may have a point, but then again, Bones is a rocker—he probably fancies this style."

"What about a hot new pair of jeans instead?" Victoria asked as she wandered over to a display. "These are super." She showed Sarah a funky pair of boot-cut red velvet pants with a sprinkling of rhinestones around the waist.

"Yum," Sarah agreed as she reached out a hand to feel the sumptuous material.

"Do you have these in a smaller size?" a familiar voice called out from the other end of the shop.

"I say, isn't that Phillipa Ainsley?" Victoria whispered as she craned her neck to see who was speaking.

"The very same," Sarah said as she looked over Victoria's shoulder. Phillipa Ainsley was turning back and forth in front of a full-length mirror. She wore a superior expression on her face and a pair of jeans that were at least two sizes too small for her.

"Can you believe she's asking for an even

smaller pair?" Sarah giggled. "I must say, if I looked like that in a pair of trousers, I'd lose some weight *tout de suite*. How could Bones McCall possibly be interested in her?"

"Shhh!" Victoria admonished. "She'll hear you!"

No sooner were the words out of Victoria's mouth than Phillipa spun around and glared at Sarah. "Why, if it isn't little Sarah Pennington." She spat the words out. "How positively enchanting to run into you."

"On the contrary, Phillipa, I'm afraid that the pleasure's all mine." Sarah glared back.

Phillipa twirled in front of the mirror. "I've been fearfully busy," she simpered as she admired her reflection. "I'm afraid I had to spend the morning at the palace. The prince is home for a few days, and Wills absolutely insisted that I drop by."

"Of course." Sarah gritted her teeth. She didn't believe for a moment that Prince William was interested in Phillipa. Wills would choose Sarah over Phillipa any day!

"But then, all the men that you're dangling after seem to find me so much more—er, how shall I say this?" Phillipa cocked her head and examined Sarah as if she were a particularly loathsome species of insect. "So much more *fanciable*."

74

She nodded in satisfaction and spun back to admire herself in the mirror.

"Don't even bother to respond," Victoria whispered in Sarah's ear. "She's not worth it."

"She may not be," Sarah whispered to Victoria. "But I can't let her get away with that!" She eyed Phillipa. "That outfit will look perfect for my Saturday-night date with Bones."

Victoria gasped, and Phillipa whirled around once more. "That's a bloody lie!" she sputtered. "There's absolutely no way that Bones would date you! He's mine, he is—you keep your claws off him!"

"Afraid that you can't handle the competition?" Sarah cocked an eyebrow at Phillipa.

"There is no competition," Phillipa said stiffly. She turned toward the clerk who'd been hovering anxiously in the background. "Charge these to my account." She indicated the jeans she was wearing as she swept imperiously out of the store and into the Rolls-Royce that was waiting at the curb.

"Well!" Victoria exclaimed. "Haven't you dug yourself into something of a hole? I mean, you *don't* have a date with Bones on Saturday."

"That remains to be seen, doesn't it?" Sarah said in a cocky voice. "Just because I don't have one now doesn't mean I won't by then."

"That's true," Victoria said. "But Sarah, what if he doesn't even show up at school before then? I mean, how are you going to get him to ask you out if you don't even meet him?"

"Oh, I'll think of something," Sarah said with more confidence than she felt. "I'll think of something, just you watch."

Either that or I'll move to Australia, she thought with a sinking feeling in her stomach.

The MI5 agent pressed his lips together as his hated German foe forced his knife ever deeper into his ribs. "Ve have vays of making you talk," the SS officer hissed, his tone one of pure menace.

"That's the one thing you don't have," Miles Langham the Third, gentleman scholar, heir to a dukedom, and secret agent extraordinaire, said in a tightly controlled voice. "You may have cunning, you may have daring, you may have the whole power of the German Wehrmacht at your back, but you have no way of making me talk. I will give my life before I give away my country's secrets, you scoundrel. . . ."

"This is bloody drivel," Max exclaimed in disgust as he threw down his pen and leaned back to scan his jottings of the last forty minutes. He cringed as he read over the last few sentences. Of course the German spy hissed in a tone of pure menace. Would he be likely to hiss in a friendly fashion? Shaking his head, Max leafed back through the last five pages, his heart sinking as he did so.

Just as he suspected, the whole lot was nothing more than a waste of paper. *Absolute rubbish*, he thought with a frown as he crumpled the paper into a wad and tossed it into the bin at the far end of the room.

Max couldn't understand how the good ideas in his head came out so dead and dull when he put them on paper. *Maybe I should be using the computer*, he half joked to himself. He reached into his desk drawer for the folder where he kept the first fifty pages of his manuscript.

The first part isn't too dreadful, he thought as he skimmed the pages that he'd written months ago. True, there were plenty of clichés and quite a few logistical howlers as well—it was hard keeping track of just how many different types of fighter planes Germany had—but still, the thing had an energy, a zest, that he couldn't seem to capture anymore.

Max placed the folder back in the drawer and leaned back in his chair with his hands laced behind his head as he pondered the reasons why his writing had gone so completely to hell.

It was because he was so confused, he realized with a deep sigh. He didn't have the mental energy to deal with his writing when he was so caught between his feelings of duty toward Lavinia and his deeper emotions toward . . .

Elizabeth!

His heart jumped as he caught a flash of her bright hair in the garden below. What was she doing? She appeared to have some sort of book under her arm. Max lifted the window sash and leaned out as far as he could, intent on seeing even more of her.

She was sitting on one of the ancient stone benches that dotted the estate. The one she'd chosen happened to be Max's favorite, situated as it was underneath a giant cherry willow. The willow bore no blooms, but Max couldn't help thinking how romantic she looked with the long, sweeping branches forming a perfect frame for her golden beauty.

You've got it bad, mate. He couldn't help grinning at how fanciful his thoughts were. He knew if Lavinia were sitting under the tree, his reaction would be very different. He'd probably be thinking that it was time for Davy O'Malley to cut the branches back. Of course, Lavinia wouldn't be caught dead sitting on one of the stone benches— she'd be too afraid of snagging her silk stockings.

Max knew that he should shut the window. He should shut the window and get back to his story; better yet, he should focus on his thesis. But even as he told himself to back away from the window, he found himself leaning out even farther, fascinated by her every movement. As he watched, Elizabeth flipped open her book and began writing.

Her journal, Max thought as he devoured her with his eyes. It was clear that Elizabeth wasn't suffering from writer's block. The words seemed to flow out of her effortlessly. Max hungered to know what she was writing. Did he figure in her thoughts as much as she did in his? He longed to talk to her about the craft of writing. What would she think if he showed her his first fifty pages? He knew that her opinion of his book would matter to him more than just about anyone else's.

I'm marrying another woman in a month, he thought guiltily as he ran his hand through his hair. *Shouldn't I care more about her opinion? I should just shut the bloody window and back away. Think about my bride to be—forget I ever saw Elizabeth.*

Max slammed the window shut with as much force as he could muster and flopped back down in his chair. He pushed the pages of his novel aside and drew his heavy economics text toward him.

Who am I kidding? He shook his head in dismay. He'd read the same sentence for the past five minutes, and he couldn't begin to understand what it said. The words seemed to dance on the page.

Maybe I need a tea break or something, he decided, stretching his hand toward the intercom. *No,* Max thought, shaking his head. He didn't want any tea; he wanted the person who would be *serving* the tea.

I shouldn't be doing this, he thought, jumping out of his chair and hurrying from the room. *I'm absolutely crazy. Not only am I engaged to another woman, I'm supposed to be meeting her in less than an hour!*

Max slowed his pace down to a stroll as he walked out onto the lawn and made his way to where Elizabeth was sitting. It was one thing to sit and talk to her but quite another to look like a complete lovesick fool. *Even if that's what I am.*

"Hey," he said as he dropped down on the grass in front of the bench. He hugged his knees to his chest and smiled up at Elizabeth.

"Max!" Elizabeth exclaimed. She seemed startled for a moment, but she recovered herself and flashed Max a brilliant smile.

"I was having an awful time trying to write, when I looked out the window and saw you scribbling away like mad—" Max gestured toward Elizabeth's journal, which lay on her lap. "I couldn't help feeling a bit jealous, and I wondered if you might have a cure for writer's block?"

"I wish," Elizabeth murmured, blushing slightly, and Max wondered if she was flattered or bothered by the fact that he'd been watching her. "If it seems like I was having an easy time writing, it's because I *was* just scribbling." She closed her journal and placed it on the bench beside her. "Just some private thoughts. Believe me, if I had a paper due or was trying to work on a book, it would be a different story. Sometimes I've spent an hour trying to come up with one sentence." She pushed a stray lock of long blond hair back into her ponytail and smiled at Max.

"My problem's a little different," Max admitted. "I hear everything so perfectly in my head, but by the time I get it down on paper, it's changed somehow. Or maybe it was bad to begin with, I don't know. I only know that when I read over what I've written, I can't help being shocked by how dreadful it is."

"Is this your thesis that you're talking about?" Elizabeth looked interested. Her blue-green eyes sparkled with curiosity, making her look even more beautiful.

"No, I'm afraid my thesis would sound dreadful

in my head as well, not just when I put it down on paper." Max grinned wryly. He stared deeply into Elizabeth's eyes for a second. Should he tell her about his thriller? They'd talked about writing a few times in the past, but he'd never told her much about the novel. He wanted to talk about it so badly, wanted to be able to share his hopes and dreams with someone, and he wanted that someone to be Elizabeth.

Max cleared his throat nervously. Somehow taking to Elizabeth about his secret writing project seemed even more intimate and forbidden than sharing a kiss. But as he looked at her, he knew that he had to share his innermost self with her. He had to give her a part of himself that was hers alone. Even if he was pledged to another woman, he wanted to share something deeply personal with this one. "The fact is—" He paused and raked his hand through his hair. "Well, the fact is, I've been working more on my novel than on my thesis. It's a spy story, actually. Very cloak-and-dagger, you know, a James Bond sort of thing."

"Tell me the plot!" Elizabeth said, staring expectantly. She looked so interested!

Max told her all about his spy and the German foe. Elizabeth seemed to drink up every word. She dropped down on the grass beside him as he talked, told her everything about his spy and where Max seemed to be blocked as a writer.

He was amazed at how easy it was to talk to Elizabeth and how understanding she was. No, *A spy story, how perfectly ridiculous. Now do stop fretting over nonsense and help me choose the flower arrangements.* No, *A spy story? What rubbish. How will that help you in Parliament?* Just complete acceptance.

"I've thought about trying my hand at a novel too," Elizabeth admitted as she stretched her slim legs out in front of her. Max couldn't help noticing how shapely they were even under the baggy chinos she wore as part of her uniform, and he wondered what she looked like in other clothes. He realized that he'd never seen her out of her drab Pennington House outfit, and he had a sudden vision of them on a date, Elizabeth dressed in some floaty chiffon thing, a flower in her hair. Did she dress like that? Somehow Max didn't think so. Elizabeth wouldn't go in for frills like Lavinia, but whatever she wore, he knew she would look stunning.

"There are quite a few mystery magazines in America—I don't know if they have them here," Elizabeth went on, oblivious to Max's daydreams. "They publish short stories. It always seemed like a good way to break into getting published."

"I'm afraid I'm a long way from that," Max said, dragging his thoughts back to the topic at hand. "If I can't do any better than I am now, I may just bag the whole thing."

"Oh, no, how can you say that?" Elizabeth looked genuinely dismayed. "Maybe you're having a bad spell now, but so what? We all do. The important thing is not to give up."

"Yeah, okay." Max shrugged. "But what about the fact that what I'm churning out is utter rubbish?"

"Maybe you just need a change," Elizabeth offered. "You need to focus on something different for a while so you can go back to your book with a fresh eye."

"Perhaps," Max said, intrigued. He plucked a blade of grass from the immaculate lawn and began chewing on it thoughtfully. "The problem is, I can't think of what else to focus on."

"How about your thesis?" Elizabeth rolled over on her stomach and propped her chin in her hands. "I know you say that you can't stand working on it, but"—she paused and smiled at Max—"by the time you've spent a few hours on it, you'll be dying to get back to your thriller. I bet the words will just pour out of you."

"You know something?" Max said slowly. "You may just have hit on something brilliant. In

84

fact, the best times I've had working on the book have been when I've been completely exhausted from trying to tackle my stupid thesis."

"It's the same with me." Elizabeth nodded. "I used to work at a newspaper, and whenever I'd get really blocked on a story, I'd start in on some statistics homework. After wrestling with something like that for a while, I couldn't wait to get back to whatever story I was supposed to be writing."

"You worked on a newspaper?" Max was startled. "Good Lord, I must say, I *am* impressed."

"Oh, it was just the campus newspaper." Elizabeth made a dismissive gesture. "Really, it was nothing."

"It still sounds impressive," he said encouragingly, hoping she would continue and tell him more about herself. He wanted to ask more pointed questions, such as what campus and where. What was the name of the paper, and what did she do before she showed up at Pennington House?

Max was dying to know about Elizabeth's past, but he was too well-bred to pry. Still, he couldn't help hoping that she would decide to share some personal details with him the way he had with her. Couldn't she tell how close he felt toward her? Was it all in his mind? Did she find their conversation as helpful and interesting as he did? Did she even remember the one kiss that they'd shared?

"Elizabeth," he began tentatively. "Do you think you could tell me . . ."

"Max." Elizabeth spoke at the same time. She seemed to be struggling with something inside, and Max wondered if her thoughts were running along the same lines as his.

Maybe she wants to tell me all about herself, but she's just being sensible, like I should be. Maybe she's just protecting herself. After all, she knows as well as I do that this can lead nowhere; she knows that Lavinia and I . . .

Lavinia! Max looked at his watch. He'd come dangerously close to missing his appointment with her, and now he'd have to rush like mad if he wasn't going to be late. He hated to tear himself away from Elizabeth, but there was nothing he could do about it.

"I'm sorry, Elizabeth." Max's voice was filled with regret. "I have to dash into town—an errand, I'm afraid." He couldn't bring himself to tell her the real reason he had to go, but from the look on her face it was clear that she had a strong inkling of just why he had to leave.

"I understand," Elizabeth said. She turned her head slightly so that Max couldn't see her face.

Max sighed deeply. He wanted to take her in his arms, tell her how much he enjoyed talking with her. *Hell, I just want to do anything but leave her and spend the rest of the afternoon picking out bloody silver patterns!*

But Max knew that he wouldn't do any of the things that he wanted. He would do what was expected of him instead.

I don't have the courage to do what I really want, he thought disconsolately as he walked slowly to his car. But he couldn't help wondering as he slid behind the wheel and started down the drive whether or not doing what was expected of him was going to end up breaking his heart.

Chapter Five

"Only five pounds, miss, and it would look absolutely fabulous on you."

"No, thank you." Vanessa smiled regretfully as she put the wildly patterned turquoise dress back into the bin. "I don't have five pounds."

After leaving her mother's old flat, Vanessa had decided to cheer herself up by wandering over to the Portobello flea market. The market was world famous and a considerable tourist attraction, but plenty of Londoners frequented it too, and Vanessa was one of them. She'd often gotten amazing deals on some fabulous vintage clothes.

They may be tatty, Vanessa thought as she held a 1940s-style rayon floral dress against her slim figure. *But they do have a certain style.* She walked over to a dusty cheval mirror that was draped with beads and studied her reflection.

"I'm no judge of clothes, but I'd say that you looked stunning," a familiar voice whispered in her ear.

Vanessa stiffened. The mirror showed two reflections; standing behind her and smiling in an altogether too familiar way was James Leer.

"You," she said, whirling around, her face a mask of fury. "What are you doing following me?"

Did James follow me to Mum's? Vanessa shuddered at the thought. If he saw the abject poverty that she'd once lived in, he'd be sure to conclude that she'd been stealing from the earl.

"I'm not following you," James said, taking a step back as if to emphasize his point. "I happened to be shopping here myself, and I saw you. And Vanessa—" His voice dropped several octaves. "Can't we be friends? Must you always look at me as if I'm the enemy?"

You bloody well are the enemy! Vanessa glared at him. She wanted to say the words out loud, but she held them back—she couldn't afford to antagonize James too much, not when he held her future in his hands. If he reported her to the earl before she found the evidence . . .

"I—I was just shocked to see you," she said lamely. "After all, what is one of the wealthiest men in the kingdom doing at a flea market?"

"That's easy." James flashed her a charming smile. "I'm looking for a gift for my mother."

"Of course." Vanessa's tone was sarcastic. The bitterness that she was trying hard to contain flared up as sharply as before. She hated it when rich people went slumming. Of course Vanessa *had* to buy her clothes at the flea market, but James could easily afford to buy out Harrods' entire stock. "I'm sure your mum's just pining away, waiting for the perfect cracked vase or the most stained tablecloth that you can find. Spare me, James." She made to push past him.

"No, really," James insisted, hurrying to catch up with her. "My mother would be absolutely crushed if I bought her some fancy meaningless gift from some exclusive Knightsbridge shop. She's quite an original. That's why I think the two of you would get along."

Vanessa stared at him. Was he making fun of her, or was he serious? The intensity of his expression convinced her of his sincerity, and she cursed him inwardly. *Why, when I want so badly to hate him, does he have to go and say something sweet?* Vanessa didn't want to like James, but sometimes he made it very hard not to. She better get away from him—she didn't want to chat with him and give him an opportunity to sway her with his charm.

"Well—" She crossed her arms in front of her chest and fixed James with a hard stare. "Your mum *may* be an original, but something tells me that we wouldn't exactly get on. Mothers of well-to-do eligible young men rarely like girls like me. I'm sure she'd be much more interested in your lady friend of the other night."

"My God!" James went white, and Vanessa realized that she'd hit her mark. She'd insulted him—perhaps more than she intended to. She nodded soberly and prepared once again to move past him.

James's arm shot out and stopped her. "Do you realize that's the first complimentary thing you've ever said about me?" he said with a shocked expression on his face. "You think I'm eligible! Besides that, you're jealous!"

"I am not jealous!" Vanessa exclaimed hotly, but she couldn't help giggling at the expression on his face. "And as far as your being eligible . . ." She softened. "That would seem to be the opinion of most women, but before you get a swelled head, let me remind you that it's your bank account they're thinking of, *not* your personality."

"Not only did you just compliment me, but you're smiling!" James moved even closer to study her face. "This *is* a historic moment. I think we should celebrate! Would you have lunch with me, Vanessa?"

Vanessa paused for a second, unsure of what to

do. James's arm felt strong as it lay across hers. How would it feel, she wondered, to rely on that strength instead of always running away from it? Vanessa had carried the burden of her mother's sickness and death alone for so long, she knew that it would feel infinitely comforting to have someone to lean on. . . .

But that someone could never be James! She wrenched her arm away. How had she let herself be lulled by his soft voice and gracious manners? He was a rich playboy, just like the earl. He wasn't seriously interested in her—he just wanted to toy with her. He was only *seriously* interested in girls of his own class—like that one with the too tight jeans who she'd surprised him with the other night.

Besides, who really knows what he's up to? Vanessa thought as she stared at James, her eyes shooting fiery sparks. For all she knew, he was plotting to tell the earl what he'd seen. Perhaps his wanting to take her to lunch was just a ploy; maybe he just wanted to pump her for information so he could strengthen his case when he went to the earl.

I should ask him what his game is, Vanessa realized. After all, she never had found out on that ill-fated trip to Oxford. She should demand to know what his plans were—but she was suddenly too nervous to ask.

"Will you have lunch with me?" James asked softly. "We could start fresh. I'm willing to forget that you've made it pretty clear that you don't want anything to do with me if you're willing to give me the chance to flirt like mad and try to charm you to death."

An image of sitting in a tony bistro with James, talking and laughing, flashed through Vanessa's mind, but it was immediately replaced with a vision of her mother lying drunk and passed out in a filthy hovel. *I can't have lunch—or anything else—with him!* Vanessa vowed.

"No!" Vanessa exclaimed, using both hands to push James away from her. Even if she wanted to, she simply couldn't afford to get involved with him. She had to stay focused if she was going to avenge her mother.

Besides, Vanessa thought as she plunged into the crowd, *even if he really does care for me, even if it would feel heavenly to have his strength to lean on, he'll hate me soon enough—as soon as I destroy the Penningtons, he'll hate me.*

Vanessa was dimly aware that James was racing after her, but the crowd was an effective deterrent, and she was outpacing him. She turned around once to look and could barely see his tall blond figure through the throng of people.

Well, that's that. Vanessa nodded to herself.

She'd lost him. *I should be relieved,* Vanessa tried to convince herself. *I should feel relieved,* she repeated firmly. *So why do I feel worse than ever?*

"Well, Max, what do you think, the Eau de Nile or the linen white?" Lavinia held up two samples for his inspection.

"Hmmm?" Max was so bored that he could hardly see straight. He'd dashed into London to meet Lavinia on Bond Street, only to find that the errand that she had insisted was so important was nothing more than a trip to the stationers'. Max sighed deeply. He could barely bring himself to listen to what she was saying. His mind was still back in the garden with Elizabeth. Instead of the stationery that Lavinia was showing him, he saw Elizabeth's face, and instead of hearing Lavinia's voice prattling on about vellum or silk finish, he heard Elizabeth intelligently discussing the problems that a writer faced.

"Max," Lavinia said impatiently. "Are you listening?"

No! Max shook his head in an attempt to clear his mind. He really had to start paying more attention to Lavinia. "I'm sorry, Lavinia." He made an effort and was rewarded by one of her rare and beautiful smiles. "What paper do you prefer?"

"Hmmm." Lavinia furrowed her brow, turned

back to the paper samples, and considered them as seriously as if the fate of the British royalty were written on them instead of meaningless samples of calligraphy. "Of course the linen white is classic, but I think the Eau de Nile is more elegant."

"Of course." Max nodded. He had no idea why they were even ordering stationery. Hadn't they arranged for their wedding invitations ages ago? His heart sank as he thought of all those snowy white cards propped up on mantels across Britain. How he wished that they'd never been sent! "Uh, Lavinia? Why exactly are we choosing this paper? It's not for thank-you notes, is it?"

"Max!" Lavinia looked shocked, and her eyes widened. "Of course not! Our thank-you cards were made to match our wedding invitations." She shook her head as if she was amused at how silly he was being. "This is our family stationery; why do you think I'm having both our crests engraved on it?"

"I see." Max nodded. "Did we really have to take care of this today?"

"Max!" Lavinia exclaimed in horror. "It will take at least a month to have the stationery made up, and I couldn't think of getting married without it! Can you imagine living together without having the proper stationery with which to respond to invitations?"

"Of course not," Max murmured. *Hasn't she ever heard of e-mail?*

"Well, I, for one, vote for the Eau de Nile, with the copperplate in navy." Lavinia looked relieved at having made the decision, and Max made an effort not to let his eyes glaze over.

Finally the stationery was chosen, ordered, and paid for, and Max and Lavinia left the store. "What do you say we get some tea?" Lavinia asked as they wandered down Bond Street. "We could nip into Fortnums."

Max had no desire to sit in the overcrowded tearoom of Fortnums, where they were sure to run into Lavinia's friends, and in any case he was supposed to meet James for lunch in an hour or so. But even if he hadn't had an appointment with James, he wouldn't have wanted to have tea. He and Lavinia were near Hatchards, his favorite bookstore, and he would much rather go in and browse through the stacks than sit in an uncomfortable chair, munching on miniscones.

"Sorry, Lavinia." Max spread his hands in a gesture of regret. "I'm meeting James in about—" He paused for a second. "Well, actually, in about twenty minutes." Max felt terrible lying to Lavinia, but he had to get out of there. "I had no idea it was so late. Do you think we can do Fortnums later?"

"I wish you'd told me, Max," Lavinia said

stiffly. "You seem to be getting quite forgetful these days. I hope it's because you have your thesis on the brain," she added pointedly, staring at him.

"That's exactly it," he told her, not even caring now that he was lying. "Look, I'm sorry, Lavinia—" He squeezed her arm. "I'd better get going."

"Fine." Lavinia sighed. "I'm meeting Callista at Harrods later anyway. I might as well get a head start on picking out my stockings. It's quite possible that I'll have to get a custom color especially woven to go with my wedding dress."

"Of course." Max nodded wisely. He didn't have the slightest idea what she was on about.

"Well, then, I'll be seeing you later." Lavinia leaned forward, and Max dutifully pecked her on the cheek.

I'm free! he thought as he watched her elegant, slim figure negotiate the crowded streets as she made her way toward Knightsbridge and Harrods. *Free—well, for the next hour anyway.*

Max walked the few blocks to Hatchards with a spring in his step. He pushed open the door and smiled at the saleswoman who greeted him with a discreet nod. Even if he hadn't been the earl of Pennington's son, they would have recognized him—Max was one of the store's most faithful customers.

Hmmm, what do I want? Max asked himself as

he ran his hands over a complete set of Dickens. He pulled out one of the handsome leather-bound volumes and flipped through the pages. It was a good edition of *A Tale of Two Cities*, but he'd already read it; besides, the library at Pennington House was fully stocked with at least ten different copies. Max put the volume back and wandered into the back room, where the modern fiction was displayed.

He studied the glossy hardcovers that were laid out on an elegant inlaid table. The latest prizewinners were there, along with an impressive selection of thrillers—Max wondered if he should read some for inspiration with his own work, but nothing really appealed to him.

Maybe I should . . . What's this? His eye was suddenly caught by a particularly colorful cover. The scene was a photo montage of what appeared to be a beach in southern California. One of the girls splashing through the surf reminded him so much of Elizabeth that he had to look twice to make sure it wasn't her. Max knew that Elizabeth was from southern California—it was about the only thing he did know about her past—and he wondered if she would like the book. He wanted so badly to give her a token, something that showed her how much she meant to him. He opened the book and flipped through it; it was a collection of short stories by one of Britain's newest and brightest talents.

I bet Elizabeth would love this, he thought as he laughed out loud at the witty dialogue. Max closed the book and glanced at his watch. If he dashed like a madman, he could get to Pennington House and still make it back in time for lunch with James. Maybe Elizabeth would still be in the garden. His heart raced as he imagined the look on her face when he handed her the gift.

"Would you like it wrapped, sir?" the clerk asked as he handed over the slim volume.

"Yes, actually," Max decided. "But if I could just have it back a second? I'd like to write something inside."

"Certainly." The clerk smiled and handed the book back.

Max drew his Waterman pen out of his pocket, but he couldn't bring himself to write with it. It seemed wrong somehow to inscribe a gift for Elizabeth with a pen that Lavinia had bought him. He shook his head and gratefully accepted the ballpoint that the clerk offered him instead.

Let's see—Max frowned. *What can I possibly say?*

He paused for a second, and then it came to him.

Elizabeth—if circumstances were different.

> *Love,*
> *Max*

* * *

"How am I going to get close enough to see him, let alone get him to ask me out?" Sarah grumbled to Victoria as they stood in the hall outside the lunchroom. They'd cut their shopping trip short and returned to Welles, only to have to push their way through a mass of photographers and reporters at the gates. Clearly Bones McCall was in residence.

Sarah had been thrilled at first—as far as she was concerned, victory was in plain sight. All she had to do was introduce herself to Bones and chat him up for a few minutes, and the rest would take care of itself.

Now, however, things didn't seem so easy. Oh, Bones was there, all right, but he was surrounded ten deep by groupies.

"He's so hot!" Victoria exclaimed as she craned her neck to get a glimpse of him.

"Oh, he is smashing," Sarah agreed. "At least the side of his nose that I can see. Look," she growled, grabbing Victoria's arm. "There's Phillipa!"

Both girls stared as Phillipa boldly pushed her way through the throng and into the inner circle. Once there, she sidled up to Bones and looked at him with an expression that made Sarah positively sick. "Careful, Phillipa, you don't want to drool all over his uniform," Sarah muttered.

"Of all the cheek!" Victoria exclaimed as they

watched Phillipa elbow several other girls out of the way so that she was closest to Bones. "If she gets any nearer, she'll be wearing the same uniform!"

"Bloody cow," Sarah agreed vehemently. "You know," she said thoughtfully as she watched Phillipa's antics. "I'm not sure that she really knows him at all. I think she's having us on. Look—" She gestured at Bones, who was barely paying attention to Phillipa for all that she was simpering and grabbing at his blazer.

"I'm going to go over there." Sarah made up her mind. "If horse-faced Phillipa can barrel her way through, then I certainly can!"

"I'm coming too," Victoria agreed as they both began to push and shove their way through the crowded lunchroom.

Sarah heard snippets of conversation as she elbowed the other students aside. From the general tone of the comments it was clear that she wasn't the only one who fancied Bones. Even without Phillipa the competition would be stiff. *I just hope that I can work my magic.* She felt a twinge of nervousness as she drew closer.

"Ouch!" she cried as someone thwoked her in the ribs while another student stepped on her feet. Getting to Bones was about as bloody easy as climbing Everest, but finally she was close enough to get his attention.

He is truly snag worthy! Sarah gasped as she got a glimpse of him head-on. He was just as sexy as he'd been onstage the other night. Somehow he managed to look even better in the blue school blazer and gray flannel trousers than he had in black leather.

Sarah was about to move in for the kill when Phillipa shot out her arm and grabbed her.

She's as strong as a bloody ox! Sarah gasped as she tried to wriggle out of her grasp.

"Back off," Phillipa hissed as she increased the pressure of her grip. "He's mine, and you're *not* getting a look in."

"Afraid that if he secs me, it's all over for you?" Sarah arched an eyebrow.

"No." Phillipa smiled evilly "I'm afraid that if he sees you, he won't want to remain at Welles any longer." She let go of Sarah's arm abruptly.

Bloody hell! Sarah thought as she stumbled backward. *She'll pay for that! Bones will be mine. Whatever it takes, I'll get him away from that cow if it's the last thing I do!*

If there was only someone I could talk to, someone I could confide in. I feel so conflicted, Elizabeth thought, pausing for a second and flexing her fingers. She'd been writing in her journal for over an hour—she'd begun right after Max had left, she'd barely moved since then, and now her hand was starting to cramp.

That's better, she thought, and as the circulation started to flow, she bent her head toward her journal again.

I feel so conflicted. She wrote the words again, this time underlining them three times. *On the one hand, my feelings for Max are clear—I simply feel more for him than any other guy I've ever known. When we talk, our connection feels so deep, so pure, but then he has to run off and play lord of the manor, and I'm stuck as a scullery maid.*

Elizabeth sighed deeply as she replayed their earlier conversation in her head. She'd been thrilled to hear about the book he was working on and flattered when he took her suggestions to heart, but then he'd dashed off. *And I have a sneaking suspicion that his errand had long, blond hair and answered to the name of Lavinia,* Elizabeth thought bitterly.

Maybe I'm just setting myself up to be hurt. If only Max would just come out and tell me how he felt—however he feels, I could deal with it; I just can't stand being so unsure. Elizabeth stopped for a second and read over what she'd written. Although she'd always poured her soul into her journal before, lately it seemed to her that she was relying on it to help her over the rough patches even more than usual. Obviously she needed an outlet—especially since she didn't have anyone to talk to, but still, Elizabeth couldn't help wondering why she felt so much needier than usual.

It's like there's a cloud of sadness over me, and I just can't seem to shake it. I don't know why, but after almost five months it's getting worse—or maybe I'm just changing. Now instead of hating Jess, I'm almost starting to miss her. And Nina—I miss Nina the most of all.

Elizabeth closed her journal and leaned back against the tree. Tears prickled behind her eyelids as a wave of homesickness threatened to overwhelm her. She remembered the last time that she'd seen Nina Harper, her best friend from SVU. They'd gone shopping in downtown Sweet Valley, and Nina had . . .

"Elizabeth." Max's voice was soft in her ear.

Elizabeth's eyes flew open. She was startled to see Max's face only inches from her own. "M-Max," she stammered. "I—I thought that you were in town. . . ."

"I was." He handed her a carefully wrapped package. "I took care of my errand."

Elizabeth stared at the bright wrapping paper. "For me?" She touched the ribbons hesitantly. *Max bought me a present?* She didn't know quite what to think. He'd kissed her, then disappeared for a month, and now he was bringing her a present?

"Aren't you going to open it?" Max asked softly. He sat down next to Elizabeth. He was so close that she could feel his breath on her cheek.

"I . . . yes . . . ," Elizabeth answered, but her mind was on other things. She was acutely aware of his body beside hers. *What if I just turned to Max and kissed him now?* she wondered. How would he react? Would he be shocked? Would he respond eagerly? What if he was offended? Elizabeth's heart beat against her ribs as she ran through the various scenarios. *It doesn't matter how he'd react,* she thought as she unwrapped the package. *It doesn't matter because I'm too nervous to kiss him.* The ribbons came apart, and Elizabeth was left staring at a picture of one of the most beautiful beaches in Sweet Valley.

"I don't believe it. . . ." She was dumbfounded. She'd told Max that she came from southern California, but still. . . .

"Does it remind you of home?" Max's voice was gentle.

"It doesn't just remind me of home," Elizabeth said, swallowing hard. "It is home."

"As soon as I saw it, I thought of you. But Elizabeth." Max touched her cheek. "I wanted to give you something to show you how much I care, not something to make you unhappy."

106

"It doesn't make me unhappy." Elizabeth could barely speak.

"Then why are your eyes filled with tears?" Max asked quietly. "I'm sorry, Elizabeth, I was thoughtless. You haven't told me much about why you left home, but I get the feeling that things haven't been that easy for you. Maybe I shouldn't have gotten you something that reminded you of your past."

"No," Elizabeth said firmly. She reached for Max's hand without thinking and squeezed it tightly. "It's a wonderful present. It does make me think of home, and that does make me a little sad. But Max, I'm more happy that you bought it for me than I am sad."

"Open it," Max urged.

"All right," Elizabeth agreed. She was surprised at the tense expression on his face as she flipped open the book. *He inscribed it!* she realized with a start. Her eyes misted over once again as she read what he'd written.

"Elizabeth," Max said quietly. He intertwined his fingers with hers and looked deeply into her eyes. "All my life people have been envious of me—the only son of the earl of Pennington, heir to all this—" He gestured at the manicured lawns and the impressive house beyond. "And I've always felt incredibly fortunate. I understood that I'd inherited a position, a position that came with

107

a certain responsibility." Max was silent for a moment, and Elizabeth squeezed his hand to show that she was listening. "One of those responsibilities is marrying a girl who comes from the same world I do. I've always known that I would marry someone like Lavinia—and until you came along, I was always happy with that choice. But more than my happiness is at stake. And I can't just turn away from my obligations."

Elizabeth was speechless. She'd wanted a declaration from Max. Well, here it almost was; he was telling her as clearly as possible that he cared for her—and that their situation was an impossible one. She laughed bitterly as she remembered what she'd written in her journal just moments before. She'd thought that as long as he told her where she stood that she could handle it. *But I guess I was wrong.* Elizabeth swallowed hard. Now that Max had told her they didn't have a future, it hurt much worse than she would have expected.

What did I expect, though? It's not like it's news that he's marrying someone else! I've known that since the day I arrived.

Elizabeth nodded silently as she looked at Max. His face was so close to hers that she could see the slight stubble on his cheeks. His dark hair was slightly windblown, and he looked more dashing and handsome than ever.

I want to kiss him. I'm going to kiss him! Elizabeth decided. If they didn't have a future, at least they had the present. She leaned closer, preparing to make her move, but before she could do so, Max kissed her.

Mmmm. Elizabeth nearly swooned at the sweetness of it. She reached upward to entwine her hands around his neck, but Max had already broken the kiss.

"Elizabeth," he said regretfully. "I have to go again. I . . ."

"Never mind, Max." Elizabeth smiled sadly. "I understand."

But do I? she wondered as she stared at his departing back. *And more important, now that I know for sure that he cares for me, can I really just let him slip away?*

What the bloody hell is up with that little minx? James wanted to know, a frown distorting his handsome face as he wandered through the streets of Chelsea. He was on his way to meet Max at their favorite pub for lunch, and though ordinarily he would have welcomed the chance for a few pints and a game of darts, his mind was too filled with thoughts of Vanessa to care about anything else.

I just can't figure her out, James admitted to

himself. To say that Vanessa blew hot and cold was like saying that in London it rained on occasion. It was the truth, but it was sure stating the case a little mildly.

Of course Vanessa's usually more cold than hot, but still, today she was glacial! James shook his head in despair. *If I had any sense at all, I'd forget about her and move on. She obviously doesn't want any part of me!*

But James couldn't seem to let her go. She was much too captivating. One look into her deep brown eyes was to be lost, and while she could certainly be tricky to deal with, he couldn't help but admire her feisty personality.

James swung open the door to one of his and Max's favorite pubs and walked toward one of the back booths. Apparently he was early because Max wasn't there yet. He threw his jacket into one of the green leather booths and picked up a handful of darts by the bar.

Couldn't hurt to practice a few throws while I wait for Max, he thought as he let the first one fly. He and Max had a running competition, and so far Max was ahead by about fifteen thousand points.

Spot on! Bull's-eye! James smiled as his throw hit its mark. He signaled the barman and ordered a pint of dark ale as he rolled up his sleeves and got down to some serious playing.

He was hoping that playing darts would take all of his mental energy, but unfortunately he still had more than enough left over to obsess about Vanessa.

What does she have against me? he wondered. *Why won't she trust me, and what the bloody hell was she doing in the countess's suite that night?* James thought back to when he had surprised Vanessa as she was leaving the countess's private sanctum. It seemed that her animosity toward him had intensified since then.

She must be afraid that I'll give away her secret, but I don't even know what her secret is! He shook his head in confusion and let loose with another dart.

Could Vanessa be stealing money from the Penningtons? James refused to believe that. Vanessa might be a tad temperamental, but she clearly was a person of integrity.

Could she be having an affair with the earl? James went cold at the idea. No. There was simply no way. Even if Vanessa had been willing, James was sure that the earl wouldn't take advantage of a young woman who was dependent on him for her livelihood.

Still, something's not right, James knew as he picked up his tankard of ale and swallowed half of it. *I just wish I could figure out what.*

"Please don't tell me that you're engaged in some futile attempt to try to beat me at darts," Max said, interrupting James's train of thought as he slid into the booth.

"Futile?" James gestured at the dartboard. "Sorry, mate, but by my count I've scored no less than six bull's-eyes while you no doubt have been loafing around town, picking china patterns."

"China patterns?" Max hooted as he took a swig of James's ale. "Have you taken leave of your senses? We picked out china patterns months ago. Now we're on to our home stationery."

"Home stationery?" James quirked an eyebrow at Max. "I take it Lavinia doesn't approve of e-mail?"

"E-mail?" Max shuddered. "Of course not; terribly déclassé. But enough about me and my woes. Tell me, have you made any progress with Vanessa?"

"Depends what you call progress," James replied as he threw another dart. This one went wide of the mark. "Damn! You seem to have a bad effect on me." He gave Max a lopsided smile as he threw the handful of darts on the table and slid into the booth. "But in answer to your question, I suppose you could say that things *have* progressed with Vanessa: They've gone from bad to worse." He grabbed the tankard from Max, took a long swig, and signaled the bartender for another.

"Sorry to hear that," Max said. He picked up the menu and scanned it for a few moments. "Anything you want?" He raised his eyebrows at James.

"Well, I guess I'll settle for a toasted cheese," James said halfheartedly. *But what I really want is some straight answers from Vanessa about what she was doing inside your mother's suite—that's after I kiss her silly, of course!*

Chapter Six

Elizabeth pulled the covers around herself more tightly as she snuggled in bed. She'd woken up before the alarm clock, but she didn't think that she could fall back asleep. In any case, she loved waking up earlier than the other two girls it gave her the illusion of privacy for a short time at least, even if she wasn't alone.

But although she usually cherished the few moments she had to herself, this morning she was feeling too sad to really enjoy them.

Why am I feeling so bummed? Elizabeth asked herself as she flopped over on her back and stared up at the ceiling. *Is it the weather?* She frowned as she listened to the raindrops pattering down on the roof. A rainy day meant that she'd be stuck inside the house and wouldn't be able to take her breaks out in the garden.

So what? she thought. *Besides, after five months here, I'm used to the rain.*

Could it be that I haven't seen Max since that last kiss? she wondered. Although she was definitely confused about the Max situation, she could honestly say that wasn't what was keeping her from falling back asleep.

Why am I so sad? Elizabeth asked herself. *Not only did we have the most rapturous kissing session, but he gave me such a beautiful present.* She sat up, reached under the bed, and drew out the book that Max had given her.

Elizabeth stared at the dust jacket with a dreamy expression on her face. She was amazed that Max had given her a book with a photo of one of her favorite beaches back home on the cover.

Home—that's what's making me so sad. Elizabeth furrowed her brow in confusion. Sure, she was sad about the fact that she was thousands of miles from home and on the outs with her family, but what else was new? Why did it seem that her circumstances were affecting her more than ever?

Elizabeth put the book aside and reached under the bed for her journal. She needed some serious introspection if she was going to figure out what was going on with her. Lately it seemed like she never had enough time to put her thoughts down on paper, and Elizabeth thought that some time alone with her journal might be just what she needed to figure out why she was blue.

Elizabeth flipped open her journal and uncapped her pen. *Omigosh!* She gasped as she looked at the date. No wonder she was feeling so down! It was going to be Thanksgiving in just a couple of days!

How could I have forgotten something so important? she wondered. Tears welled in her eyes as she thought of past Thanksgivings; her family had always had a big celebration. Right now her mother was probably busy picking up the cranberries and buying sausage for the stuffing. Jessica was probably dashing around campus, handing in last-minute papers, and her father was probably kicking back and watching football in between being sent out on errands by her mother.

Are they thinking of me at all? she wondered. *Do they miss me, or are they just angry because I've never gotten in touch with them?*

Elizabeth chewed on her pen for a moment as she considered what they might be feeling. All the time she'd been in England, she'd never really thought about what her parents were going through. She'd felt so betrayed by them, so hurt, that she couldn't imagine getting in touch with them and telling them that she was okay, but now she wondered if she'd been a little harsh.

Mom and Dad must have been worried sick, Elizabeth thought guiltily. Would it really have hurt her so much if she'd let them know that she was alive?

And what about Jessica? Has she been worried about me too? Does she miss me, does she remember the way things used to be?

Elizabeth closed her eyes and let the memories wash over her. She pictured herself back in Sweet Valley, waiting in the Jeep while Jessica finished packing. She smiled as she remembered last Thanksgiving. Jessica had insisted on taking two entire suitcases even though they were just going home overnight. *Actually, for Jess that wasn't so bad. Remember that time she took those five-inch heels on a camping trip?*

Elizabeth was surprised that when she thought of Jessica, she felt only sadness—the anger seemed to have dulled. *I guess that means I'm healing,* she thought. *Maybe I should get in touch with them.*

No. Elizabeth shook her head. She was healing; she wasn't already *healed*. She needed more time, but at least now she could think of getting in touch with her family without bursting into tears.

Elizabeth slid the journal back under the bed. It was time to get up and get on with the day.

Vanessa and Alice were already starting to stir. Elizabeth hopped out of bed and grabbed her bathrobe.

"Can I use the bathroom first?" Vanessa asked grumpily. Her beautiful face was distorted by an unhappy expression. She whisked past Elizabeth toward the bathroom that they shared.

"Sure," Elizabeth said as Vanessa slammed the door behind her. She tried to shrug away Vanessa's rudeness, but she was irritated. Vanessa always took extra long in the bathroom, and now Elizabeth wouldn't be able to shower until after breakfast. *But I guess I should be used to her behavior by now,* Elizabeth thought. *Besides, she looks like she has a lot on her mind.*

Ha! Elizabeth laughed as she dragged her brush through her hair. She *has a lot on her mind? Like I don't?* She shook her head as she slipped on her uniform and prepared for the day ahead.

What was that? Vanessa froze in her tracks, sure that someone was following her. She looked over her shoulder, half expecting to see the earl in hot pursuit. *Nothing. You have nothing to worry about. Mary instructed you to dust along the hallways, and that's exactly what you're doing. So stop worrying!* She breathed a sigh of relief as she sagged against the wall, clutching the feather duster against her chest.

119

Vanessa started creeping stealthily down the hall again. She was bound and determined that nothing would sway her from her chosen path. She didn't care if a thousand mice ran after her—nothing would stop her because today, finally, she was going to steal the key to the earl's desk. There were a few drawers that were locked. And Vanessa had a feeling what she sought was in those locked drawers.

It had taken a lot of planning to get this far. Vanessa wasn't usually assigned to dust the earl's bedroom; that was Mary's job. But Mary was having a phone conference with Niles Neesly, so she'd given the task to Alice.

Thank God that Alice is so dim-witted, she didn't question why I was so willing to do her work for her, Vanessa thought, smiling. She couldn't wait to get into the earl's private sanctum without having to sneak in. For once.

What won't *I find there?* Vanessa's smile deepened. She was sure that the keys to his locked drawers would be there, but who knew what other goodies might be laid out for her viewing pleasure? Perhaps her mother wasn't the only one who saved letters.

As soon as I— "Aaah!" Vanessa let out a little gasp. There, in front of her, emerging from the earl's bedroom, was Max. *What if he suspects something?*

Vanessa turned white. She had no idea how to defend herself. She clenched her fists in anger—she was so close, she couldn't let things fall apart now.

"Just borrowing some cuff links," Max said cheerfully as he fiddled with his sleeves.

Vanessa was silent. She didn't give a toss about his stupid cuff links; she just wanted him to get out of the way so she could get on with her search.

"Vanessa," Max said, looking at her closely. "Are you all right? You look as if you've seen a ghost."

"I'm fine," Vanessa said stiffly. She had to mind her manners with him. After all, he was the son of the lord of the manor, and unless she wanted to be fired *tout de suite*, she better be polite to him. "I'm fine," she repeated, resisting the urge to push past him. "Thank you for your concern." She waited to see if he had anything else to say, but Max seemed to have more important things on his mind. He smiled and walked past her, whistling a jaunty tune.

At last! Vanessa felt a surge of excitement as she opened the door to the earl's bedroom. *Where to start?* she wondered as she looked around at the enormous master suite. Where would the earl be most likely to leave the keys to his desk? Where would he be most likely to leave anything of a personal nature?

He would hardly be likely to keep the keys to his desk in his antique canopied bed, Vanessa thought as she stripped the four-hundred-thread-count sheets. What about the Queen Anne mahogany dresser? Vanessa walked over and gave it a cursory dusting.

No keys here, she thought with a sinking heart. Where else could he possibly keep them? Heaven forbid that his keys were with him! What if he had them in his trouser pocket right now?

His pockets! Vanessa whirled around and stared at the trouser press that stood in the corner of the room. She dashed over and grabbed the fine wool pants from the stand. As she did so, something fell out and landed on the floor with a loud thud.

There, lying on the cool marble, winking up at her, was the earl's golden key chain.

"This chicken stock is definitely *not* up to scratch!" Mary frowned as she took another taste of the fragrant soup that was bubbling away on the stove. "Really, Matilda, you can do better than that."

Matilda turned an angry shade of red, but she didn't answer back, at least not directly. Instead she turned to Elizabeth and gave her an earful.

"Well, if Elizabeth could be bothered to chop the vegetables a little more carefully, I'm sure that it would make that much difference to the stock. And if Alice could *sweep* the floor, instead of just tickling it with the broom, then I'm sure I wouldn't have to be doing *her* job as well, and I could concentrate more on my cooking!" Matilda finished in an aggrieved tone.

"Elizabeth," Mary said sharply as she rinsed her spoon and placed it in the dishwasher. "Matilda can't do her job properly if you don't help her properly, and Alice," she continued severely, "your work is not at all as it should be, my girl. Now, I don't want to frighten you too badly, but the wedding is only a month away, and anyone not doing their work at a high enough standard will be let go."

Gee, I'm crying already, Elizabeth thought sarcastically as she began to peel a mountain of carrots. *You mean I might lose the opportunity to work for a pittance and get to wait tables at the wedding ceremony of the guy I love while he marries another girl?* She looked at Alice, intending to share a secret smile, but it was obvious that the other girl was terrified by Mary's threats.

"Y-Yes, ma'am," Alice stammered. Elizabeth was surprised that she didn't drop into a curtsy. "I'm sure that I'll do my very best, ma'am."

"See that you do," Mary said curtly as she swept out of the kitchen. She turned at the door and looked back at Elizabeth. "I didn't hear any promises from you, Elizabeth, but I'm sure that you intend to do your very best, now that you know the consequences."

Oh, brother, Elizabeth thought, rolling her eyes. *Like losing this job is the worst thing that could happen to me. Who needs to see Max getting married anyway? I don't want to watch while he—*

Elizabeth froze suddenly, the vegetable peeler tumbling from her hands, and she stood stock-still as if she'd seen a ghost. Maybe she didn't want to see Max get married to another girl, but she did want to *see* him, and if she didn't work at Pennington House, then she wouldn't be able to.

Then again, why do I want to torture myself when he'll never be mine anyway?

She shook her head in dismay. She knew why she was torturing herself. Because when all was said and done, married or unmarried, Max was just plain wonderful, and Elizabeth had never felt this way about anyone else. *And maybe I never will again!* she thought sorrowfully.

Elizabeth was overwhelmed by a wave of futility. On the one hand, she felt closer to Max than ever—after all, he'd just given her that wonderful gift. On the other hand, his wedding date was drawing closer and closer.

I can't take it anymore! I'm so confused, I have to talk to someone or I'll burst! Elizabeth buried her head in her hands.

"Elizabeth!" Matilda exclaimed. "Are you ill?"

"Yes, yes, I am, actually." Elizabeth lifted her head and looked at Matilda with a strained expression on her face. "I . . . I need a break, some fresh air, I think. . . ." She headed for the door that led out into the garden.

"Well, of course," Matilda said doubtfully. "You look as if you could do with a short rest."

Elizabeth didn't even hear her as she flung open the door and raced out across the lawn. The cool November air was refreshing after the stifling atmosphere of the kitchen. Dead leaves swirled around her feet as she ran, and the wind whipped her hair into a froth.

Where can I go? Elizabeth wondered. She wasn't sure what direction to head in, but some part of her mind clearly knew because she found herself running toward the bench where Max had given her his present.

She collapsed on the stone bench and buried her head in her hands again. Elizabeth could feel the hot tears prickling behind her eyes, and she let out a sob. For so long, she'd been so brave. Ever since that night that she'd fled the States, she hadn't allowed herself to break down. She had to focus on keeping it together. For the first few months she was too concerned with survival to let herself fall apart, but now she was at the breaking point.

What's happened to me? she thought as the tears started to flow. *Where's my life going? What will I do when Max gets married? Will I ever see my family again?* The questions tumbled through her mind.

Suddenly she felt a pair of strong arms enfold her, and a soft voice whispered in her ear.

"Elizabeth, what's happening? Tell me, let me help you."

Max. Elizabeth turned her tearstained face toward Max. He looked so beautiful, so strong and capable, that she couldn't help collapsing against him. She was dimly aware that he was stroking her hair, but she was too overcome to notice much else. She burrowed into his chest, and his arms tightened around her. As unhappy as she was, Elizabeth couldn't help feeling somewhat comforted by the warmth and caring that Max was providing. She felt a blinding flash of jealousy for Lavinia. What must it be like to know the sanctuary of his arms on a regular basis? What must it be like to be able to be held this way whenever you desired? To kiss him whenever you wanted?

It must be like heaven, Elizabeth decided. The realization that that luxury would never be hers only made her cry harder.

"Elizabeth—" Max's voice was tenderness itself. "If you want to talk about it, I'd be honored to listen. You know that I care for you—won't you let me help?"

Max's voice was too gentle, his arms were too strong, and the depth of caring in his eyes was too powerful for Elizabeth to resist his plea. She lifted her head and tried to dry her eyes with the back of her hand. "I . . . I would like to talk," she managed to hiccup.

"Let me help with that." Max smiled as he took a monogrammed linen handkerchief from his pocket and dried her eyes for her.

"Thank you." Elizabeth sniffed, than laughed as he wiped her nose for her too. "I'm afraid I don't know where to start," she said lamely. Of course, she could always start with what her feelings for him were, but she was too timid to do that.

"Well, let's begin at the beginning, shall we?" Max suggested sensibly. "How did you end up here anyway? I've often wondered how you came to be miles from home, without friends or family. Are you an orphan, Elizabeth?" His voice became even more tender, if possible, as he continued to stroke her hair.

"No." Elizabeth shook her head. "But I might as well be."

"Did you run away?" Max asked.

"I guess I did," Elizabeth confessed. She looked up at him as the tears started to flow again.

"Well." Max stopped stroking her hair to dab at her face with his hankie once more. "Do you want to tell me how that came about? I don't want to pry, but I do want to help."

"It's such a long, painful story." Elizabeth drew a long, shuddering breath. "But you're not prying, Max; I want to tell you." It was true, she realized. She wanted Max to know everything about her. She wanted to share her innermost thoughts and feelings with him— even if it was her fate to lose him to another woman, she wanted this time with him to be without barriers.

"I guess I should start with the fact that I'm an identical twin." She smiled briefly. Nobody, not even Max, could ever understand what that meant. Nobody could understand the closeness that was possible between two people who were entirely different, yet exactly the same, the way she and Jessica were. And nobody could understand the depth of pain that she was still feeling all these months later at Jessica's baffling betrayal.

"You can't possibly expect me to believe that there's another girl out there who's as beautiful as you," Max said. "I must say, though, I've always been fascinated by twins—what's it like being one of a set of two?"

"Different," Elizabeth said. She snuggled closer in Max's arms as she thought about how best to tell her story. "Also I should tell you that before I came here, I'd been offered a scholarship to the University of London's creative-writing program, but I was debating whether or not to accept."

"The University of London? Good Lord!" Max pulled away from her slightly so that he could study her face. "I'm impressed. I know what program you're referring to, and it's extremely prestigious. I would have accepted in a flash." He frowned slightly as he pulled her close again. "Why were you hesitating?"

"Because I thought I was in love with someone back in Sweet Valley. That's my hometown," Elizabeth added. She could feel a sudden tension in Max, and in spite of everything, she couldn't help feeling a little thrill. Was he jealous of the idea of her being in love with someone else? *Little does he know!* Elizabeth took a deep breath and plunged ahead with her story. "If I'd stayed in

America, I'd be in the middle of the first semester of my junior year at Sweet Valley University."

"Are you still in love with this someone?" Max asked in a tight voice.

"Sam, his name is Sam, and no, I'm not in love with him," Elizabeth said firmly. "Even if I hadn't caught him making out with my sister, I wouldn't be in love with him anymore. I thought it was serious, but it really wasn't." *Not like my feelings for you,* she added silently.

"You caught him having it off with your very own sister?" Max's expression was one of pure horror. "My God, I don't know who I'd hate more, him or her."

"Having it off, what a totally English expression." Elizabeth laughed softly. "But you're right, I didn't know who to hate more—at least back then I didn't. . . ." She paused as a vision of Sam and Jessica locked in each other's arms flashed in front of her eyes. Somehow, now that she was locked so securely in Max's arms, the image didn't pain her nearly as much as it usually did. "Anyway, now that I've had a long time to think about it, I can honestly say that Jess hurt me more."

"Jess?" Max interrupted. "I take it that would be your sister's name?"

"Jessica." The wind was starting to pick up,

and she shivered a little. "And by the way, as I'm sure you might have guessed, my last name isn't Bennet. It's Wakefield, Elizabeth Wakefield."

"It suits you better than Bennet," Max said with a smile of understanding. Elizabeth tried to flash him an answering smile of her own, but her teeth were chattering too hard. "Getting cold?" Max asked softly. He tightened his grip so that she was totally enveloped in his arms; it would have been impossible for them to be any closer. His voice was like a warm caress against her cheek, and Elizabeth could feel his heart beating against hers.

"No, I'm fine now. . . . How could I be cold when you're holding me so tightly?" Elizabeth asked boldly. She looked up into Max's eyes. The intensity she saw there nearly took her breath away. Suddenly all her past misery was forgotten. The only thing that mattered was being with Max. Sam? Who was Sam? Some guy she knew in a past life? For that matter, who was Jessica? Elizabeth had never felt such a yearning, such a hunger to kiss anyone as she had at that moment.

"I only hope that it feels as good for you to be held by me as it does for me to feel you in my arms," Max said quietly.

Kiss me! Kiss me! Elizabeth was dying to say the words out loud, but she couldn't bring herself to.

131

"I . . . it feels wonderful to be held by you," she said instead. But inside, her mind was reeling. She'd never experienced anything as extraordinary as being held in Max's embrace.

If it feels like this to be in his arms, what would it feel like to really *kiss him? To make love with him?*

"So I'm still not clear on how you ended up at Pennington House," Max interrupted her train of thought. "Not that I'm complaining, mind you."

"Um, from Sam and Jess having it off, to Pennington House—that's a pretty grim tale, let me tell you. Not that I'm complaining about being here either," Elizabeth added hastily.

"So let's hear the rest of it," Max said, resting his chin on her hair.

"Well, we'd been driving cross-country when this all happened. After I caught them, I knew that I couldn't possibly continue on as though nothing had happened. I don't mean continue the trip; I mean continue on with my life in Sweet Valley."

"An understandable reaction," Max murmured against her hair. "If I were in the same situation, I don't know how I'd be able to go on."

"I knew I couldn't go home to Sweet Valley and SVU, where I'd risk running into them on campus all the time. The motel we were staying at was only about an hour from O'Hare International Airport. I had the acceptance letter from the University of London burning a hole in my pocket—coming here seemed like my only available option."

"But Pennington House isn't the university." Max smiled. "What happened to make you give up your place at the university?"

"It gave me up." Elizabeth laughed rucfully. "I spent my last penny getting to England. I mean it—when I arrived at the school, I had only a couple of pounds, cash and credit combined. But I thought everything would be okay. I had a scholarship, a stipend, and room and board. There was just one little problem. I'd forgotten to reply to the university's acceptance letter. They'd given my place away to someone else."

"Good Lord!" Max pulled away slightly so that he could look her in the face. "You must have been at wits' end! Why didn't you just call your parents at that point? I know that I would have turned tail and fled back home on the first available plane."

"I would have, except for the fact that I wasn't talking to them either. Unbelievably enough, they seemed to have taken Jessica's side. God knows what all she told them about what really happened, but she got to them before I did, so that was that." Elizabeth shuddered as she remembered the scene at the airport with her parents. She only hoped she never had to live through anything like that again. Her parents had wanted her to come home, to apologize to Jessica for stranding her at the motel. They hadn't even considered she'd had good reason to leave Jessica. They'd been so angry at her for being *un*-Elizabeth-like. That was what hurt the most. She'd discovered that her parents hadn't known her at all.

"My God, what did you do when you found out that your place had been taken?" Max sounded horrified. "I wish I'd been there to help you, Elizabeth," he said, his voice dropping to a whisper. "I hate thinking of you so lost and helpless, though something tells me that you'd never be helpless."

"Well, I certainly felt pretty helpless back then," Elizabeth admitted. "I wandered through the city, trying to find a job, a place to sleep, anything. I spent the whole day just walking, walking, walking from one disaster to the next. Finally when I was afraid that I would have to spend the night on a park bench, I found myself on the grounds of Pennington House." Elizabeth looked around her. It was hard to believe that this had been her home for the past five months. When she'd first arrived, she'd been overwhelmed by the size of the place—she'd never guessed that it was a private home.

"I thought it was a bed-and-breakfast." Elizabeth laughed. "I was hoping that if I promised to wash dishes, I could have a bed for the night. Instead I got a job. Mary was looking for a scullery maid, and I was only too willing to sign on."

"You are so incredibly brave." Max sounded awed. "Truly, Elizabeth, you're simply unbelievable. I couldn't imagine surviving in the same circumstances. I'm so impressed by you."

Elizabeth tried to shrug off his words, but they meant too much to her. After everything that she'd been through, his praise was like a long, cool drink of water after months in the desert. "It means a lot to me that you think so highly of me," she said quietly.

"Highly of you?" Max held her face in his hands as he stared deeply into her eyes. "That doesn't begin to describe it. Elizabeth, you're the most beautiful, brave, gutsy woman I've ever had the privilege of meeting."

"Max, I—," Elizabeth began, but she was cut off as Max suddenly crushed his mouth against hers. Elizabeth entwined her arms about his neck as she returned the kiss with every fiber of her being.

Mmmm, so this is what it feels like to kiss Max. . . .

Rational thought fled as she molded her curves against his hard, muscular chest. Their kiss deepened, and it was impossible to tell where she began and he left off. Elizabeth felt like she'd been waiting her whole life for this one moment. She . . .

"Elizabeth!" Mary's voice floated out from the kitchen. "Elizabeth, where are you? We need you in here!"

Reality intruded, and Elizabeth pulled away in shock. Max looked as surprised as she did, and Elizabeth couldn't tell whether or not he was regretting what had just happened. She got to her feet unsteadily. "I—I—need to get back," she stammered.

"Elizabeth . . ." Max got unsteadily to his feet. "I . . . I . . ."

"Elizabeth!" Mary called again. "Where have you gotten to?"

"I have to go; I'll get in trouble," Elizabeth said.

"Of course." Max seemed to recover himself. He reached out a hand and touched her cheek.

Elizabeth caught his hand. Before she could stop herself, she pressed a kiss against it. Then she turned and fled back across the lawn toward the kitchen.

Is he following me? Elizabeth looked over her shoulder. No. Max was standing very still, as if he was too stunned to move.

How did that happen? Elizabeth wondered as she arrived breathlessly at the kitchen door. *And what does it mean for our future? Do we even have a future, or does the future belong to Lavinia?*

"I must say, the fresh air seemed to do you a world of good," Matilda remarked as she slid a tray of biscuits into the oven. "Perhaps you ought to take breaks like that more often."

Fine by me! Elizabeth couldn't help smiling as she picked up the peeler and returned to the carrots.

Chapter Seven

"I can't even get within ten yards of him," Sarah wailed as she and Victoria sat in the lunchroom. She'd been trying to get close to Bones for the past couple of days, but things weren't going very well. So far, the nearest she'd come to getting to know him better had been reading the fan page that several of the girls in the lower form had printed up.

"How am I possibly going to wrangle a date with him," she muttered, glancing over to where Bones was sitting, surrounded as usual by a throng of groupies. "I haven't even had a chance to introduce myself!"

"It does seem rather difficult," Victoria said sympathetically as she took a bite of her crumpet. "Maybe you should just forget about Bones."

"And let Phillipa win? Not on your life." Sarah

shook her head emphatically. "Just look at her—" She gestured with her can of soda to where Phillipa was sitting, smack in the middle of the groupies, staring at Bones with a cowlike expression on her face.

Why does she have to have such a big chest? Sarah thought bitterly as she watched Phillipa laughing and thrusting her voluptuous body at Bones. Sarah looked down at her own chest and sighed. *Maybe an American-style Miracle Bra would do the job,* she thought in desperation. *Oh, what does it matter what I wear!* Sarah grimaced. *It's not as if I'll ever get him to notice me anyway! If I could just get him alone, away from all those people!*

Lightbulb! Sarah sat bolt upright. "I have it!"

"Hmmm?" Victoria raised an eyebrow. "What are you on about now?"

"I just need to get Bones alone," Sarah said excitedly. "Once I get him away from all those awful groupies, I know that I can snag him."

"Maybe so, but how are you *going* to get him alone?" Victoria looked skeptical.

"Just you watch," Sarah said, smiling mischievously. She whipped out her cell phone and dialed directory inquiries. "Could I please have the number of the Kingsworth Hotel?" she asked as she reached over and grabbed Victoria's crumpet.

"Hey, that's mine," Victoria protested. "What

do you need the number of the Kingsworth for anyway?" She made a feeble swipe at the crumpet. "Are you meeting Lavinia there or something?"

"No." Sarah munched the last bite of the crumpet. "I'm meeting *Bones* there." She punched in the number for the Kingsworth.

"Bones?" Victoria's jaw dropped. "And just how are you going to wrangle that one?"

"Hang on a tick—" Sarah held up her hand. "Hello, Kingsworth? Hello, this is Lady Sarah Pennington. I'd like to book your best suite for this afternoon. Hmmm, yes, that sounds all right. Yes, that should do nicely. Room twelve. Yes, I should be there at about four-thirtyish."

Sarah smiled at Victoria as she pressed the disconnect button and dialed yet another number. "Hello, is this the Welles School?" Sarah pitched her voice so that it was completely unrecognizable. "I have an important message for Bones McCall. Would you tell him that he's to meet his manager, Benny, at the Kingsworth Hotel, suite twelve, at five o' clock? I'm afraid that it's terribly important. Could you see that he gets the message? Thank you ever so much." Sarah rang off and beamed at Victoria.

"You're bloody brilliant!" Victoria exclaimed in admiration.

"Aren't I just?" Sarah nodded. "Want to head

141

over to Janet Reger with me?" She quirked an eyebrow at her friend.

Victoria looked at her quizzically. Janet Reger was where the most sophisticated royals bought their undies. "Why are you rushing about trying to buy knickers anyway?"

"Not knickers." Sarah grinned wickedly. "A Miracle Bra."

"Looking for a little figure enhancement?" Phillipa Ainsley said acidly as she passed by the table where Sarah and Victoria were sitting. "I'd say that the situation's pretty hopeless." She looked at Sarah's chest, then smothered a laugh.

"Oh, I don't know," Sarah managed to say calmly, even though she was so angry that steam was coming out of her ears. "I wouldn't totally give up hope, Phillipa. I've heard that some of those figure shapers that the Queen Mum wears can take positively *inches* off one's thighs. If I were you, I'd look into those before I tried lipo."

"Laugh all you want!" Phillipa snarled as Victoria and Sarah collapsed in giggles. "But we'll see who's laughing a month from now, when Bones McCall escorts me to the Pennington-Thurston wedding." She spun on her heel and marched away. "How did a twit like you manage to get such a divine brother anyway?" Phillipa called over her shoulder.

"Bloody hell!" Sarah murmured as she stared after Phillipa's departing figure. "Bones will be at my brother's wedding, all right," she vowed. "But he'll be my escort, *not* Phillipa's!"

"Of course, we *could* always use sterling-silver roses, but Lavinia is afraid that they might clash with the bridesmaid dresses, and I'm not sure that I don't agree with her." Niles Neesly, the wedding planner, adjusted his glasses as he looked at Max for agreement.

"Yes, right." Max nodded as if he cared. He took a sip of tea, more to avoid answering any more questions than because he was thirsty. He'd spent the half hour in the library, listening to Niles drone on about the most absolutely boring things. Who cared whether the napkins were linen or damask? Who cared whether the caviar was Russian or Iranian? *In fact,* thought Max as he crossed and uncrossed his legs uneasily, *who cares about the bloody wedding at all?*

"I'll take up the flowers with Lavinia," Niles continued. He looked disappointed at Max's lack of input. "She needs to bring me swatches from the bridesmaids' dresses before we can come to a final decision." Niles jotted down a few notes on his pad.

"Of course," Max murmured. He tried to look

interested, but he was fighting a losing battle. He couldn't care less about all the stupid details of his wedding. Even if he hadn't kissed Elizabeth in the garden so rapturously yesterday, he wouldn't have wanted to listen to Niles prattle on.

That's not true, he realized. *If I were getting married to Elizabeth, I'd be excited to talk about our wedding plans, but then again, if I were marrying Elizabeth, I'd be excited about everything.*

Max closed his eyes and did his best to block out Niles as he droned on. How could he think about going through with the wedding when he was so besotted with another girl? It wasn't fair to him, it wasn't fair to Elizabeth, and God knew, it wasn't fair to Lavinia either.

I have to tell Lavinia the truth, Max realized suddenly. He couldn't go through with it. He simply couldn't go through with the wedding. It would be an absolute farce—there he'd be in front of man and God, pledging his troth to a girl he didn't love while the girl he did dished up the bloody caviar.

Max nearly groaned aloud as he considered what Lavinia's reaction would be. He hated to hurt her, but wouldn't he be setting her up for even greater misery if he wed her when he didn't love her?

Maybe in the end he'd be doing Lavinia a favor.

Max hoped that she would see it that way too, but what about his father? For years his dream had been to see a match between the Penningtons and the Thurstons. He'd all but ordered Max to propose to Lavinia. What would he say?

But what about me? Max wanted to scream. Instead he smiled mindlessly at Niles as he handed him a heavy book of silver patterns to look through.

"I thought that we could use the Malmaison style for the salmon and continue with the Odiot for the rack of lamb," Niles suggested. "Of course, Lavinia will want to have the final say, but you can have absolute confidence that she'll pick the most appropriate choice. I must say—" He gave a little laugh as he polished his glasses. "Lavinia has the most exquisite taste. So many of the young brides nowadays have so little sense of form." He shuddered. "You wouldn't believe what the countess of Denby wanted for *her* wedding. But I mustn't go telling tales out of school!" He smiled at Max.

Of course Lavinia knows what kind of ice cream forks to pick, Max thought morosely. *But is that any reason to spend the rest of my life with her?* Briefly he pictured what his wedding would be like if he had his own way. *For one thing, the bride would be different!* Max couldn't help smiling. He was sure that his wedding to Elizabeth would be

145

wonderful—lighthearted, carefree, and fun. Perhaps they'd even have it on a beach, maybe a beach back in Sweet Valley, although the south of France was nice too. . . .

"And your decision is . . ." Niles looked at Max with an expectant expression on his face.

"I think Hawaii sounds good," Max said dreamily.

"Hawaii?" Niles knit his brow. "I'm afraid I don't recall that pattern." He made to take the book back from Max.

"Sorry." Max shook his head. "I was thinking about something else. Listen, Niles." He got to his feet. "Do you mind terribly if we continue this another time?" *How about never?*

"Of course not," Niles said agreeably. "But if you could come to a decision before we meet again, that would be most helpful. You see, time is growing short, and I would like to place the orders."

"Oh, I'll come to a decision, all right," Max said grimly. "In fact, I already have."

I've decided I'm not going to marry Lavinia, he thought as he walked from the room with a spring in his step.

I can't believe that I'm actually doing this, that I'm actually on the threshold after so many months! Vanessa's hand shook as she fitted her own long-ago stolen key in the lock to the earl's study. It stuck for a second, and her heart nearly stopped, but she jiggled it, and the door swung open smoothly.

This is it! The inner sanctum! Vanessa walked in the room, half expecting the earl to jump out at her, but the room was empty, and she breathed a huge sigh of relief before plopping down in a burgundy leather club chair.

Vanessa frowned as she looked around the large, well-appointed room. Could that ornately carved chest of drawers be concealing a safe? What about the bookcases that lined the walls? Could some incriminating evidence be stuffed into one of those hand-tooled volumes?

Her eyes roamed the room as she considered likely hiding places, but there were so many possibilities, her heart sank. The locked drawers weren't the only places to look. She'd searched this room before, but if she could find that photo or a letter from the earl to her mum or a journal, even . . .

There's evidence of the affair in this stupid mansion, Vanessa reminded herself. *You saw it with your own eyes. And you'll see it again if only you get to looking, girl!*

For so long, she'd been living on the hope that she'd be able to find the photo she'd seen, but now that she'd penetrated the inner sanctum, she felt overwhelmed by doubt. Had she forgotten where she'd put it back? No. Impossible. The photo hadn't been there when she'd looked for it again. Was someone on to her? And now that James had caught her in the countess's suite, were the Penningtons simply waiting to pounce on her? Were they watching her through a hidden camera right now?

I'm such a bloody idiot, Vanessa thought with a sneer. *Those Penningtons aren't smart enough for that! And I'm being paranoid! Mary was probably dusting around and straightened up his papers and the photo got hidden between or behind some papers. Mary's such a stupid cow that she'd never even notice that wasn't the countess in that photo.*

Vanessa studied the desk carefully. The smooth leather top offered nothing, and she quickly moved to open the center drawer, which was unlocked.

Nothing but rubbish in here, Vanessa thought as she rifled through assorted stamps and paper clips. Mary had definitely tidied up this room; things were slightly out of place. Vanessa noticed a roll of polo mints and popped one in her mouth before slamming the drawer shut in frustration.

She moved quickly to the other drawers. There were two sets of three, flanking the center, and she was through with them in no time.

Nothing here. Vanessa swallowed her disappointment. She started to close the drawer, but the chain bracelet she wore caught on something, and she got stuck.

Just my luck! she cursed. Caught like a deer in a trap! What if she couldn't get free? She could just imagine the look on the earl's face when he came home to find her attached to his desk drawers.

Vanessa struggled to loosen her bracelet. *What's it caught on anyway?* She frowned in irritation as she jiggled her hand back and forth. Suddenly her hand sprang free, and as it did so, a compartment in the back of the drawer opened up.

Yes! Vanessa raised her hand in a victory salute. She hadn't come upon this one before! She was sure that she'd happened upon a treasure trove. She withdrew a fairly large manila envelope and looked at it curiously. *What could be in here?* she wondered as she opened it up and peered inside.

It was stuffed to the brim with photos, and her heart beat faster as she shook them out onto the desk. *That looks like Venice,* Vanessa thought as she leaned forward to study the pictures. *Why the earl would want to keep snaps of Venice I can't . . . Oh my God!* Vanessa's jaw dropped.

The earl had kept pictures of Venice, all right, but not just for the views of Saint Mark's Square. He'd kept them because of how beautiful Vanessa's mother looked.

Vanessa rifled through the sheaf of pictures. In some her mother appeared alone, smiling at the camera. In some she appeared with the earl.

149

Vanessa was shocked at how blissful they both seemed. In all of the snaps that they were in together, they were either kissing or hugging. The earl looked different than she had ever seen him. Admittedly he was nineteen years younger, but there was something else too—he looked incredibly happy.

Why did he leave her if he was so much in love with her? Vanessa wondered. *Because she wasn't from the same social class?*

Vanessa swallowed hard to keep from crying. The pictures were breaking her heart. There was something so tragic about how young and beautiful her mother had been, and Vanessa couldn't help comparing the way she looked in the photos with the way she'd become—a drunken, wasted wreck of a woman.

I'll make him pay for this, Mum, she thought as she shoved several of the pictures into her apron pocket. Vanessa swept the rest of the pictures back into the envelope, and as she did so, a faded piece of paper fell out. *What's this?* Vanessa thought as she scooped it up.

My dearest love, the letter began. Her heart quickened as she scanned the paper. The letter was almost better than the pictures had been. Her eyes widened as she read the earl's declarations of undying love. *I will always love you,* she read. *No matter what happens, I won't let anything stand in our way. Our love will conquer all obstacles. . . . With love forever, your beloved.*

Finally. After all this time, she had him. She had a note in his own handwriting! She had more than just some photos! She had him!

Her elation died down as she reread the love note from the earl to her mother. How could things have ended so badly? Vanessa furrowed her brow in confusion. She was thrilled that she had found such incontrovertible proof of her paternity, but she couldn't help feeling upset too. It was baffling that things had turned out the way they had. But Vanessa was determined that no matter how badly things had gone for her mother in the past, no matter how badly the earl had treated her, she was going to make sure that he confessed to what he'd done. And she was going to make sure Max and Sarah heard every horrible word.

"Careful!" Elizabeth exclaimed as Alice tried to balance a rare and valuable crystal decanter along with several cleaning implements and some silver filigree candlesticks on a very small tray. "Here, I'll take that." She smiled at the other maid as she took the decanter from her and placed it carefully back on the sideboard. Alice was sweet and hardworking, but she did have a tendency to break things.

Sometimes Elizabeth felt like she spent as much time cleaning up after Alice's spills and mishaps as she did cleaning Pennington House itself.

But at least picking up after Alice gives me something to do, Elizabeth thought as she wiped the decanter and gave the sideboard a final swipe with her dust cloth. *At least that way I won't spend all my time obsessing about Max!*

But Elizabeth knew that no matter how much work she had, she'd still find time to obsess about Max. She'd probably obsess about him for the rest of her life. Their interlude in the garden the day before had been one of the most passionate, incredible, exciting things that had ever happened to her, and she didn't think she'd forget it in a hurry.

But what happens now? she asked herself for the thousandth time. In her heart of hearts, she didn't really believe Max could kiss her that passionately if he didn't have serious feelings for her. But just how serious were they? Were they serious enough for him to call it off with Lavinia, or was he just toying with her?

Elizabeth sighed deeply as she followed Alice out of the dining room and toward the library. No matter how often she asked herself the same questions, she still didn't have the answers.

Max! Elizabeth's heart stopped as she caught a glimpse of him through the French doors in the library that opened out onto the lawn. He was standing with Niles Neesly as the other man prepared to get into his Mercedes.

Niles Neesly? The joy that Elizabeth felt at seeing Max quickly dissipated as she took in the significance of the scene. *Yesterday he was kissing me senseless, now he's discussing china patterns? What's with this guy?* She scowled. Much as she loved Max, she couldn't help thinking that his behavior was just a little bit cavalier.

Elizabeth turned away from the window and joined Alice as she straightened the chairs and picked up the sterling-silver tea service that had been left in the library. *Obviously Max was entertaining Niles in here—how cozy,* she thought sadly as she gathered up the exquisite Queen Anne pieces. She'd just as soon have tossed them out the window.

"Is something wrong, Elizabeth?" Alice looked at her with a dismayed expression on her face. "The way you're banging that tea service gave me quite a fright."

"Sorry, Alice." Elizabeth flashed her a brief smile. "No, nothing's wrong." *Correction, everything's wrong, but there doesn't seem to be anything I can do about it!*

"Because you know, if anything is wrong, I'd be only too happy to help," Alice said as she plumped up the cushions on the chesterfield sofa.

"Thank you, Alice." This time Elizabeth's smile was sincere. It was too bad that Alice was so, well, so *limited*. Elizabeth hated to be a snob, but she just couldn't see discussing her problems with her. Still, she had to talk to someone. She was in serious need of an old-fashioned girl-talk session, the kind where you sat up all night, eating junk food, with your hair in curlers while you talked about guys.

Elizabeth closed her eyes as a wave of homesickness washed over her. What wouldn't she give to be sitting cross-legged on Nina's bed, digging into a bowl of popcorn? Nina was a terrific listener. Not only that, but she usually had terrific advice. *Too bad she isn't around,* Elizabeth thought wistfully.

"Are you two finished in here?" Vanessa's sharp voice intruded on her thoughts as she came into the room.

Boy, she looks about as good as I feel! Elizabeth was shocked at Vanessa's appearance. The girl was as white as a sheet, and her mouth was set in a hard, thin line. *What happened to her?* Elizabeth thought with a surge of sympathy. *I wonder if Vanessa would be into talking,* Elizabeth considered as she studied her more closely. Vanessa's cheeks were tearstained, and Elizabeth couldn't help thinking that the other girl probably needed a confidant as much as she did.

"Because if you don't need any more help, then I'm off for a few hours," Vanessa announced as she spun on her heel.

So much for the heart-to-heart! Honestly, you'd think that I'd have learned by now. Elizabeth grimaced.

"C'mon," Alice said cheerfully. "Matilda said that there was an awful lot of crockery left in Sarah's and Max's rooms—why don't we head up there? I'll take Max's room," Alice added as they headed up the stairs toward the private rooms. "Why don't you give a quick look round in Sarah's?"

"Sure." Elizabeth nodded in relief. She didn't think that she had the emotional strength to tidy up Max's room right now. She was too bewildered and confused by his contrary actions.

Elizabeth walked into Sarah's room, carefully stepping over a pile of clothes as she moved to pick up the many pieces of china that were strewn everywhere. Sarah had a serious snacking habit, and she never called to have the dishes picked up when she was done with one of her many scone attacks.

Boy, she could give Jess a run for the money, Elizabeth thought as she surveyed the mess. It had been a serious hassle sharing a room with Jessica— Elizabeth kept her clothes perfectly pressed, while

155

Jessica considered the floor a perfectly good substitute for the closet.

At least that's one thing I'll never miss about Jess. Elizabeth forced a smile as she walked over to Sarah's computer to pick up an overturned coffee cup. She noticed that Sarah hadn't logged off and that she was still online. Elizabeth wondered if she should turn off the computer, but she had no way of knowing what files she would need to save first. She paused with her hand poised over the keyboard.

Of course I could always go online. . . . The thought startled Elizabeth. She wanted to talk to Nina? Well, she could—all she had to do was type in Nina's e-mail address, and she could have a virtual pal within moments.

Should I do it? Elizabeth wondered. She couldn't believe that she was even considering getting in touch with someone from back home, but she hadn't talked to anyone from Sweet Valley for five months now, and suddenly the urge was overwhelming.

"Are you done in here?" Alice popped her head in the doorway, and Elizabeth whirled around with a guilty expression on her face.

"I . . . uh, yes, I'm done in here," Elizabeth replied, scooping up the teacups and plates and hurrying from the room.

Was I really just about to e-mail Nina? Elizabeth wondered in disbelief. Of course she never would have used Sarah's computer, but that was hardly the point—the amazing thing was that she felt like she was ready to talk to Nina. Ready to talk to—*home.* Because that's what Nina represented. Home. *My family.*

I guess I'm like E.T., Elizabeth thought with a smile. *I'm finally ready to phone home!*

Well, phone her old best friend. But it was a start.

Chapter
Eight

Vanessa took the letter out of her apron pocket and read it for the tenth time. She knew that she should hide it somewhere safe, but she couldn't resist reading it over and over again. She just couldn't get over how much in love the earl had been with her mother, and she also couldn't get over the fact that he was her father.

Of course she'd known from the first that she was his daughter, but there was a difference between knowing and *knowing*.

She walked slowly across the lawn and through the French doors to the dining room. Vanessa paused a second and stared at the long expanse of the Georgian dining table. She should be eating there, she realized suddenly, not *serving* there. Her heart ached with the injustice of it all.

Vanessa walked boldly over to one of the elegant

chairs and pulled it out. She sat down before she could think twice. *What if Mary finds me sitting here like this? Should I tell her that I have every right to be here? That I'm the earl's oldest daughter?* Vanessa couldn't help giggling. Maybe she should break the news that way.

She cocked her head as she considered how best to tell everyone. That was something she *hadn't* thought about much for the past few months. She'd been too focused on finding the proof she needed, not what she was going to do with it once she found it.

Should she just throw the pictures in the earl's face at dinner that night? Maybe she should conceal them inside one of the serving dishes. *No.* Vanessa frowned. Too theatrical by half. She wanted to be more subtle, to make the earl squirm.

"Vanessa—" Max poked his head around the door, startling Vanessa out of her reverie. "Have you seen my economics text? I can't seem to find it anywhere. I was sure that I'd left it in the library, but no luck."

Vanessa started guiltily. Would Max reprimand her for sitting down in the dining room? What if he did? Would she tell him that he had no right, that she was his sister?

His sister! Vanessa felt faint, and she gripped

the edge of the table for support. She'd never really thought about the fact that if the earl was indeed her father, then Max and Sarah were her siblings.

Max is my brother! Vanessa stared at him in disbelief. For a second she couldn't help wondering what it would have been like to grow up with him around the house. Would he have beat up on the blokes who treated her disrespectfully? What about Sarah? Would she and Vanessa have gone on shopping trips to Knightsbridge together?

Vanessa closed her eyes and imagined all the things that might have been. She imagined taking family vacations with the Penningtons. . . . *But I'm a Pennington too,* she thought desperately. Her eyes flew open, and she stared at Max again. Prosperity, happiness, companionship, all these things had been denied her. They'd been denied her before she was ever born, when the earl tossed her mother aside like so much rubbish.

"Are you all right, Vanessa?" Max sounded concerned.

"No." Vanessa shook her head emphatically. She got up and, pushing Max aside, rushed out of the room. *I'm not all right,* she thought wildly as she dashed up the stairs.

For months now she'd been searching for proof that the earl was her father, certain that when she finally found it, her life would get better. Vanessa shook her head in dismay as she climbed the last flight of stairs to the attic. She just couldn't figure out why, now that she had the proof, she felt worse than ever.

"Yes, this will do very nicely," Sarah said, nodding as she followed the porter into the deluxe suite that she'd booked. She blushed slightly when she saw the enormous bed that dominated the center of the room. She walked over to the sitting area instead of flopping down on it as she would have if she were alone.

"This is so cool!" She smiled as she sank down into one of the overstuffed down chairs opposite the roaring fire. *And very romantic too,* she thought with a slight flutter in her stomach.

Sarah stretched back against the luxurious upholstery and sighed happily. There was a huge arrangement of flowers on the mantelpiece, and the table in front of her held a basket of fruit, chocolates, and assorted sweets. She could see why this was Lavinia's favorite hotel, and she wondered if the ice sculpture and Max had ever booked one of the suites.

"That will be all, thank you," Sarah told the porter as she gave him a couple of bills from her purse.

"Thank you, madam." The porter closed the door behind him discreetly, and Sarah jumped up to inspect the bathroom.

"Ooh!" She couldn't help exclaiming at the expanse of marble tub that rivaled even her own back at home. Sarah looked at the shampoo and soaps that the hotel had provided—they were Penhaglions—the queen's favorite brand. *Too bad I didn't come for a bath!* she thought regretfully as she glanced at her watch. It was almost time for Bones to show, and she better get ready. She wanted things to be perfect.

Sarah ran back into the room and grabbed her bag from where she'd flung it by the door. She took the Miracle Bra and her hot black dress and hurried back into the bathroom. She had a little difficulty struggling into the bra—it seemed to have a thousand hooks—but finally she was done, and she slipped the black dress over her head.

Phwoar! she gasped as she stared at her new figure. *I should have done this ages ago!* The bra was indeed a miracle. Sarah had curves she'd never even dreamed of, and the black dress set them off to perfection. She brushed out her tawny brown hair until it positively glistened and then applied some mascara to her blue eyes, which were sparkling with excitement.

After she put on some sparkly, vanilla-flavored

lip gloss, she gave herself a final, satisfied glance in the mirror. Then she walked back into the bedroom, wobbling slightly on her high heels.

Time to set the mood, she thought as she reached into the bag for the scented candles that she'd bought earlier.

After lighting the candles and placing them strategically, she set up a boom box and slipped in a Bloody Young Blokes tape.

Sarah looked around and nodded in satisfaction. The candlelight flickered softly, bathing the room with a dim golden glow. The music was a little wild for the mood, but it was Bones's own group. And if the mirror over the mantelpiece didn't lie, she looked sensational.

She settled back against the couch with a contented sigh. She was ready.

Bones didn't stand a chance.

Can I do this? Max stared at the phone as if it would bite him. He'd been staring at it for the past twenty minutes. Occasionally he'd pick it up and start to dial, but he always hung up before he could complete the number.

I have to do it. He closed his eyes and massaged his temples, the pounding in his head so loud that he felt like the entire timpani section of an orchestra had taken up residence in there. *Maybe I should ring down for some codeine tablets*. He laughed hollowly. He knew that popping a few pills wouldn't be enough to get rid of his headache. The only thing that would cure the pain in his head would be if he broke things off with Lavinia.

Which is why I've been staring at the bloody phone for the past half hour, he thought with a grimace as he reached once more for the phone. He picked up the receiver and began to dial for the tenth time.

But how will I tell her? Max shuddered at the thought of how the conversation would unfold. He was sure that Lavinia would weep, and he hated the thought of that happening. Maybe he didn't want to spend the rest of his life with Lavinia, but that didn't mean he wanted to hurt her either.

Max slammed down the phone just as it started to ring. Sure, he had every intention of telling Lavinia that he could no longer see her. He just didn't seem to be able to translate *intention* into *action*.

How can I break it to her? He got up and began pacing around the room. What was the best way to tell your fiancée that you weren't in love with her? Max wished there was someone he could ask for advice, but who could he turn to? He laughed as he realized that Lavinia herself, so brilliantly

165

schooled in etiquette, would probably be able to advise him better than anyone else.

Well, one thing was for sure. He wouldn't tell her over the phone. That had to be a pretty shabby way of handling things. He'd tell her in person. Max picked up the phone and punched in Lavinia's number; this time he waited for her to pick up. Now that he'd decided he wasn't going to break the news over the phone, he felt like he'd been given a reprieve.

"Hello?" Lavinia's musical voice floated over the phone, and Max felt a wave of guilt flood over him. He hated to do this to her, but he knew deep inside that if the marriage went through, it would prove disastrous for both of them.

"Lavinia—" Max tried to sound upbeat. "Look, something rather urgent has come up. Could you get away for a bit? Perhaps meet me in town?"

"Urgent?" Lavinia sounded alarmed. "Max, it's not about the flower arrangements, is it? Niles *did* say that he could get pink peonies flown in from New Zealand. Has something gone wrong with that? Because if he can only get white, I'll be most upset. I need pink to coordinate with—"

"No, no, Lavinia—" Max cut her off. "As far as I know, there's nothing at all wrong with the flowers. It's something rather more serious. Could we meet? Say in an hour or so? Would tea suit, do you think? We never did get to Fortnums the other day."

"Hmmm, I *would* fancy a tea at the Kingsworth. Call ahead and book a table, and I'll meet you at five-thirtyish. Okay?"

"Perfect." Max nodded. He hung up and dialed the Kingsworth. His mind was in a whirl as he planned just what he would say to Lavinia when he saw her.

One thing was for sure, he thought as he made the reservation: Even Lavinia would have to admit that his news was more important than the flower arrangements.

Elizabeth put down her journal with a sigh. It was useless. There was simply no way she was going to get any writing done; she couldn't even begin to concentrate. Every time she tried to write, a picture of Max as he leaned in to kiss her flashed before her eyes.

Elizabeth wouldn't have minded that; in fact, reliving that moment was distinctly pleasant. The only problem was that the picture was invariably replaced by one of Max talking to Niles Neesly— and that was something she definitely didn't want to think about more than she had to.

I don't get it, she thought as she stretched her

167

arms above her head. *What kind of game is he playing anyway?* Elizabeth got up and began pacing back and forth in the garden as she considered the problem.

Max certainly *seemed* like a stand-up guy; one of the things that she loved most about him was his incredible sense of integrity. Would someone like that really stoop to toying with her feelings this way? But still, she hadn't seen him since their passionate embrace. Where was he? Was he avoiding her? He certainly hadn't made any effort to see her. *Maybe I'm being oversensitive, but the fact that he kissed me senseless and then disappeared is making me feel kind of insecure!*

Oh, I just can't take this anymore! Elizabeth plopped back down on the bench and ran her hands through her hair. Writing in her journal wasn't going to help. Trying to struggle through things on her own wasn't going to help. There was only one thing that *would* help.

She could talk to Max. She could confront him, challenge him, make him tell her what was really going on. She'd certainly spilled her guts with him yesterday—couldn't he at least return the favor?

Elizabeth jumped up and headed toward the house. She was incredibly nervous, but she knew that she was doing the right thing. She cared deeply for Max, and unless he was the world's greatest actor, it was pretty clear that he cared just as deeply for her. The question was, what did he intend to do about it?

How am I going to bring this up without totally losing it? she wondered as she walked through the French doors. *I have to act calm and not . . .* "Max!" Elizabeth exclaimed in surprise as she bumped into him coming out of the dining room and onto the lawn.

Was he looking for me? she wondered with a flush of pleasure. Maybe he'd seen her from his window like he had so many times before and was coming out to get her. Her heart beat faster at the thought. "Hi, Max," she said somewhat breathlessly.

"Hi, yourself." Max smiled at her, but Elizabeth couldn't help noticing that he looked somewhat distracted.

"Is something wrong?" Elizabeth asked. "You seem . . . I don't know, unhappy. . . ." She trailed off, afraid that she was being too forthright.

"No, no, nothing of the kind. Really, Elizabeth." He gripped her arms, and Elizabeth felt a thrill course up and down her spine.

"Of course," she murmured. She couldn't help feeling disappointed, though. "Perhaps we can see each other later?"

"Yes, I . . . Look, Elizabeth." Max's grip intensified, and he looked deeply into her eyes. "I have a terribly important meeting in town, but I really need to talk to you afterward. Trust me. It's most important."

"Well—" Elizabeth laughed shakily. She was stunned at how forceful he was being. "You know where to find me."

He looked at her, looked at her hard, then nodded and jogged off toward his car.

Now, what was that all about? Elizabeth wondered. Was it possible that his errand had something to do with Lavinia? Maybe he was calling off the wedding! There was no way to know, but what else could be so terribly important, and what else would he want to discuss with her later? She walked into the kitchen with a jaunty step and placed her journal on the table.

Oh, what are you being such an idiot about? Elizabeth chastised herself. *Like Max would really call off the wedding for you! You know that he has to marry Lavinia. When are you going to get over the fact that Max belongs to someone else?*

Elizabeth glanced around the room. Alice was slicing mushrooms, Matilda was up to her elbows in pastry flour, and Vanessa was nowhere to be seen.

"There you are, Elizabeth." Matilda smiled at

her as she rolled out some pastry dough. "Could you get me the Devonshire cream, please?"

Elizabeth walked over to the refrigerator and got the cream for Matilda. "Here you are," she said, smiling back. She looked into one of several mixing bowls that flanked the marble pastry board. "This looks delicious." Elizabeth eyed what looked like chocolate-chip batter. She would have loved to steal a small taste, but after five months of working in the kitchen, she knew that sort of thing simply wasn't done.

"Chocolate-chip scones," Matilda said, confirming Elizabeth's guess. "That's all young Lady Sarah ever seems to want," she grumbled. "I didn't study two years in Paris just to waste my time making chocolate-chip scones." She dumped the cream into the batter.

"Well, I think they're delicious," Elizabeth said. She grabbed a paring knife and went to help Alice with the mountain of vegetables.

"Hmmph!" Matilda snorted. "Then all I can say is that your taste is no better than hers. Now, Max certainly has a discriminating palette."

He sure does! Elizabeth grinned as she popped a green pepper in her mouth. "Shhh!" She put a finger to her lips to quiet Alice, who looked properly scandalized.

"It's a pity he won't be home for tea," Matilda

went on. "But he rushed off in a lather to meet that hoity-toity fiancée of his. *She* needed to be taken to the Kingsworth Hotel for tea, if you please. Well, that's fine by me." Matilda began dropping table-spoonfuls of dough onto a greased baking sheet. "It seems Miss Lavinia thinks that I've too free a hand with the icing sugar on the éclairs that she wants to serve at the reception. . . ." Matilda rambled on, unconscious of the effect that her words were having on Elizabeth.

He's taking her out for tea? At the Kingsworth? That doesn't exactly sound like they're on the outs, now, does it!

Elizabeth's heart sank as she replayed the conversation that she'd had with Max not twenty minutes ago. Clearly she *had* misread the whole thing. Clearly she *was* an idiot.

I just don't know what to think anymore. She shook her head sadly. Max's behavior was beyond her. The only thing she could do was wait until he came back. Then she'd hear what he had to say. She only hoped that the news was going to be good.

Chapter Nine

Sarah paced nervously around the room, teetering a little on the incredibly high Manolo Blahnik sandals that she'd bought to go with the tight black dress. She paused in front of the ornate mirror that hung over the mantelpiece and regarded herself critically.

I do look great, she reassured herself. And the room was perfect, and the music was hot—everything was in place, everything, that was, except Bones McCall.

Sarah gnawed her lower lip as she glanced at the clock. He was already ten minutes late. Maybe he wasn't coming at all. Maybe he'd figured out that the note was a fake; maybe he was laughing over it with Phillipa right now. Sarah winced as she considered the possibility.

I guess I should just forget it and head on home,

Sarah thought disconsolately as she sank into one of the overstuffed chairs and kicked off her shoes. She started to massage her aching feet and was considering changing into a pair of jeans that she'd brought with her when she heard a knock at the door.

Forget it—it's probably just housekeeping, she thought with a sigh. Still, it wouldn't hurt to look. Sarah got up and walked over to the door. She peered through the peephole, half expecting to see a maid with a handful of towels. Instead she saw Bones McCall, leaning against the wall with his hands in his pockets, looking, if possible, even sexier than he had the last time she'd seen him.

Yes! Sarah did a little victory whoop before straightening her dress and opening the door.

"Hey." Bones gave her an appreciative glance before sauntering into the room. "Where's Benny?" He frowned as he turned around the room, his eyes widening in surprise at the flickering candles.

He's so sexy! Sarah couldn't help thinking as she studied him. Bones had taken off his leather jacket and slung it over one shoulder, and she could see his lean, sculpted muscles underneath his T-shirt.

"Well, you are definitely not my ugly old manager," he said as he sat down in one of the chairs. "Did Benny send you on ahead? Or can he not make it?"

"Actually, I'm not really sure what Benny's schedule is," Sarah said slowly. "You see, I've never talked to him before."

"Huh?" Bones cocked his head. "Is this some kind of joke?" He looked at her closely for a second. "Don't I know you from somewhere?"

"It's not a joke." Sarah sat down in a chair opposite him. "And you have seen me around before. I go to Welles, but you see, we don't really know each other because you're always surrounded by groupies."

"Did you arrange all this just to meet me face-to-face?" Bones stared at her incredulously.

Sarah nodded slowly. Her heart was knocking against her ribs so loudly that she was surprised he couldn't hear it. Would he think she was crazy? Would he get up and storm out and tell everyone at school? "Yes—" She licked her lips nervously. "I *did* arrange all this just so I could get to know you."

"Well." Bones gave a slow smile. "I do like your taste in music."

Sarah beamed.

"She's got the most absolutely smashing haircut I've ever seen," gushed Alice as she swept the kitchen floor. "I'm just mad for it. Elizabeth, does everybody in America do their hair the same way?"

Oh, who cares? Vanessa snorted as she seasoned

several salmon fillets for dinner. She had too much on her mind to join in the stupid conversation that Matilda, Alice, and Elizabeth were having.

"Well, not everybody," Elizabeth said as she walked by Vanessa on her way to the refrigerator. "But an awful lot of girls do have some version of Jennifer Aniston's style, whatever style she has at the moment."

"I'm not as interested in her haircut as I am in how oddly thin the girls are on that show," Matilda said. "They're rails!"

Please. Vanessa rolled her eyes as she took the bunch of dill that Elizabeth was offering her and added it to some finely chopped and seeded cucumber. She couldn't wait to finish with the dinner prep so that she could be on her own and study the photos once more. She could hardly believe that she'd found the proof she needed. Now all she had to do was confront the earl and things would—

"Matilda?" The earl's familiar baritone cut through Vanessa's thoughts. She spun around in shock. The earl *never* came into the kitchen. Was he here because he knew what she was up to? Had James finally reported her? Or had he simply found that the papers on his desk had been messed with? *He's going to fire me right here,* Vanessa thought, her face draining of blood. *He can't, though! Well, go ahead, old man. Because I've still got the proof. And you can fire me, but I've still got the power to destroy your perfect little family!* Still, Vanessa was so nervous about what the earl wanted that she dropped the knife with a loud clatter, causing everyone to turn and stare at her.

"Ahem—" The earl glanced at Vanessa for a second, then turned back toward Matilda. "Just wanted to let you know that I won't be in for dinner. I'm dining in town with an MP tonight. The intercom seems to be a bit jammed, or I wouldn't have come down." He nodded at the staff and left the room as suddenly as he had come.

Vanessa sagged against the counter in relief. *That was a near thing!* She wiped her hand across her forehead. *What if he found out that I took the letter and photos and he knows I've got proof? I'm not ready for him to know that his secret is out. Does he suspect me? No. Why would he? Although I do look a lot like Mum. I certainly don't take after the earl!*

He's my father. My father! Vanessa clutched the edge of the sink as her knees buckled underneath her.

She'd known for months now that the earl was her father; after all, the whole reason she'd come to work at Pennington House in the first place was to confront him with that fact, but somehow she'd been so focused on finding the proof she needed that she'd forgotten she actually had a *father.*

I have a father, Vanessa thought, closing her eyes tightly to stop the tears that were threatening to overflow suddenly. *All those years when Mum and I were struggling by ourselves, all those years when the other kids made fun of me because I didn't have a dad—all those years I did!*

She tried to hold on to the sink, but she was too overcome, and she stumbled a little.

"Vanessa! Are you okay?"

Vanessa heard Elizabeth's voice, but it seemed like it was coming from a great distance. She tried to nod that she was fine, but she couldn't seem to manage even that. She clung to Elizabeth as the other girl slipped her arms around her and led her to a seat by the table.

"Matilda! Alice! Vanessa's ill!" Elizabeth cried.

"No, really, I'm fine," Vanessa managed to choke out. She felt incredibly embarrassed that she was making such a scene, but she was well and truly overcome.

"You're absolutely not fine," Matilda said, feeling her forehead. "Now, what's come over you so suddenly, poppet? The place for you is upstairs in bed. Come along now, I'll make you a cup of tea, and then it's off to bed with you." She bustled over to the stove and put the kettle on.

Vanessa leaned back in her chair and massaged

her aching head with her hands. Elizabeth and Alice were staring at her with concerned expressions on their faces, and she tried to summon up a smile to show them that she was okay. Her mouth wobbled, however, and she gave up the effort.

I'm not okay, she realized. *I'm not okay, but I will be,* she thought, accepting a cup of steaming tea from Matilda and taking a deep sip. *I will be just as soon as I confront him and make him pay for what he's done to me and Mum!*

Max drummed his fingers nervously on the table. The task ahead of him filled him with anxiety, and he couldn't help thinking that the incredibly chic, *public* lobby of the Kingsworth Hotel wasn't the most ideal place to break up with his fiancée. Still, she had chosen the place, and indulging her in this one small thing was the very least he could do.

He leaned back in the delicate Regency-style chair, upholstered in pink satin, and surveyed the lobby with a bored expression. An acquaintance waved to him from across the room, and he gave a small smile in return. Max hated the idea of others witnessing what was about to happen. Thank God Lavinia had exquisite manners—at least she could be counted on not to make a scene. In fact, now that Max thought about it, maybe meeting in such a public place was an excellent idea—the chances of either of them getting overly emotional were certainly minimized that way.

Max relaxed for a second and listened to the tinkle of the piano playing in the lounge. He was glancing at the menu when out of the corner of his eye, he saw Lavinia enter the lobby and walk toward him.

Heads turned as she moved, and Max was struck once again by how beautiful she was. He knew that most men would think he was crazy for giving her up, but he couldn't continue with the charade any longer.

"Max, sorry to be late." Lavinia pecked him on the cheek as she removed her cashmere gloves and sat down opposite him. "The traffic was absolute murder," she said as she signaled for the waiter. "And to tell you the truth, I would have been late anyway since I was having a devil of a time trying to sort out the mess that Mary Dale and Matilda Kippers have managed to make of the wedding pastries. Honestly, Max—" She ran a perfectly manicured hand through her immaculately coifed hair and sighed deeply. "I don't know how you've managed with them all these years. It must be that you don't really know what it is to have a woman's touch, but would you believe they've tinted the icing the wrong color for the éclairs?"

"Excuse me?" Max shook his head. As far as he was concerned, Lavinia might as well be speaking another language. He didn't have the slightest idea what she was on about. Worse, he didn't know how, when she was intent on talking about the wedding arrangements, he would be able to tell her there wasn't going to be any wedding. Perhaps he should just let her natter on for a few more minutes.

"I was saying that they've gotten the color of the icing wrong for the éclairs for our wedding reception, Max. Honestly, do you ever listen to anything? The help in your house is simply unacceptable." Lavinia made it sound like the Pennington staff had been found guilty of major war crimes. "I gave them a swatch of silk that I wanted them to match. I *told* them that it was absolutely essential that the icing coordinate with the bridesmaids' dresses—"

Max couldn't take it anymore. If he had to listen to one more detail about the bloody stupid wedding, he'd go stark raving mad. "It doesn't matter about the bloody icing, Lavinia!" he interrupted suddenly. *What have I done?* he thought as he watched the color drain away from Lavinia's face. Underneath her exquisitely applied makeup, she'd gone absolutely white.

"I'm sure I didn't hear you correctly, Max." Lavinia's voice was icy cold. "Because I know that the—"

181

"You did hear me correctly, Lavinia," Max interrupted her again. "You did hear me correctly," he went on more quietly. "I don't care about the icing. I don't care because I—" He ran a hand through his hair and took a deep breath. "I don't care because . . . Lavinia, I am so sorry. So, so sorry. But the wedding is off. I can't marry you, Lavinia. I can't."

Lavinia stared at him in shock as the waiter placed a cup of fragrant tea in front of her. She waved away the plate of cakes that he was offering with an imperious hand and took a deep sip of the tea. She closed her eyes for a second, and some of the color came back into her face. Max was relieved to see that she seemed to be recovering.

"Mmmm, there's nothing like Earl Grey, is there?" Lavinia commented brightly as though Max hadn't spoken at all. "I think it's the bergamot flavoring that makes it so delicious. Now, why did I say no to that plate of tea cakes? I do fancy a scone after all. Max?" She smiled brightly. "Would you mind calling the waiter back?"

"Lavinia . . . I . . ." Max was baffled. Hadn't she heard a word that he said? Perhaps this was going to be even harder than he thought.

"Oh, Max." Lavinia laughed. "Don't just sit there gaping. Be a darling and call the waiter over."

"But Lavinia—" Max cast about for the right

thing to say. "Surely you heard me? I said I was calling off the wedding!"

"Oh, I heard you, all right." Lavinia nodded absently as she signaled for the waiter herself. "You want to call off the wedding." She took another sip of her tea. "I've no doubt that you're going to get a quiver in your voice and tell me that your heart belongs to another." She narrowed her eyes over the rim of her cup. "And I'm sure that I can guess who has your eye these days—the American scullery maid, is it? Elizabeth something. Bennet, I believe. My God, Max, how incredibly predictable. The son of the earl of Pennington charmed by the kitchen maid! Couldn't you at least have been a little more original? I must say, I don't think much of your taste. She looks a bit scruffy. However, that's none of my concern. But *this* is—the wedding *will* continue. Don't think that this little flirtation will get you off the hook."

Max sat back in his chair, burning with anger. He wanted to defend Elizabeth—scruffy, indeed! But somehow it seemed like incredibly bad taste to defend the woman that he loved to the woman he was ditching. He wouldn't stoop to that. No, he'd better concentrate on what Lavinia was saying. He'd better explain to her that no matter what she thought, the wedding *was* off.

"I think you're missing something, Lavinia," Max said stiffly. "You see, I don't love you. My heart *does* belong elsewhere, and as long as that's true, I can't marry you."

"Max!" Lavinia stared at him incredulously. "Do you seriously think that my heart goes pitter-patter every time you come near?" She laughed. "Of course I'm fond of you, but don't delude yourself that I love you. Since when did love and marriage have anything to do with each other in our circle?"

"I . . . I . . ." Max was dumbfounded. Surely Lavinia shared his romantic notions? He was amazed at how coolly she was taking things.

"Oh, Max!" Lavinia bit into one of the miniature éclairs that the waiter had placed in front of her. "How can you be so incredibly naive? Our marriage will make us two of the most powerful people in London society." She eyed him. "Surely you don't expect me to turn away from all that just because you've shown the incredibly bad form of falling in love with the scullery maid?" Lavinia's eyes sparkled with a cold blue fire as she looked at Max.

"Actually, Lavinia—" Max's voice was deadly quiet. "You may well have to turn your back on all of that. You see, however much you may want to, you can't actually *force* me into marrying you."

Lavinia stared at him and smiled coldly. "Oh, but I think I can." She arched a brow.

"And just how do you intend to do that? Forget it, I don't care. Look—" Max tried to gather his thoughts. The conversation had gotten way out of control, and he was ashamed of the way he'd spoken to her a few moments ago. Maybe she was just acting this way out of wounded pride. Maybe if he didn't talk about his feelings for Elizabeth but emphasized the other reasons why they wouldn't suit, maybe then she'd accept defeat gracefully.

"Lavinia, I'm afraid that it's not just Eliz—it's not just that my feelings are elsewhere, it's that so much about me has changed this past year. I don't want to finish my thesis. I don't want to join Parliament. I want to write a novel, to be my own man, not be some boring clone of my father."

"Yes, I see." Lavinia looked bored. "That's all very well and good, but you see, Max, you *will marry me*."

"What makes you so bloody sure?" Max threw up his hands in despair.

"Let's just say that unless you marry me as planned, I'll leak a *very* embarrassing scandal about the illustrious Pennington family to the press. Think about it, Max—your father will be ruined. Your little sister won't be able to take her place in London society. This isn't just about you, Max; other people's lives are at stake as well."

"What scandal?" Max stared at her. He was well and truly baffled. "What on earth are you on about, Lavinia?"

"Let's just say that before my mother died, she told me a secret about your family, Max. Something terrible. Something that would destroy all of you, but mostly, at this point, your beloved little brat of a sister. That's all I'll say. Push me, and all of England will know the story. That's the very reason my mum told me the secret in the first place. As a sort of security system, just in case I'd need it to get what I want." With that, Lavinia stood and walked gracefully from the room.

What the hell is she talking about? Max wondered as he stared openmouthed at her departing figure. He rose to call her back, but he found himself speechless.

What family secret? What scandal?

Chapter Ten

James pulled his car into the driveway of Pennington House and hopped out of the car. He didn't have a definite appointment to meet Max, but he was driving back to Oxford and thought he'd stop at his friend's before he took off.

His feet crunched over the gravel as he headed toward the back door and the kitchen. He figured if he entered that way, instead of ringing at the front door, he might be able to catch a glimpse of Vanessa.

That way I can at least—"Vanessa!" James exclaimed. The object of his fantasies was sitting huddled on one of the many stone benches that dotted the lawn. "Vanessa?" he called. "What's wrong?"

"Vanessa?" James said softly again as he stood looking down at her. She looked even worse up close. She was as pale as a sheet and trembling like a leaf. His heart nearly melted at the sight of her in so much pain, and it was all he could do to keep from crying out.

"What happened?" he asked as he sat down on the bench next to her. Vanessa turned to look at him, and James could see that she'd been crying. "Did Matilda or Mary yell at you—was that it?" he tried, casting about for a reason for her distress.

"No." Vanessa's voice was so quiet that he had to lean even closer to hear her. "Nothing like that." She was trembling so violently that James was afraid she was going to faint. He couldn't just sit by and watch her in this pitiful state; he had to do something. James reached out to gather her in his arms. He didn't care if she pushed him aside. He simply had to hold her.

To his joy and amazement she *didn't* push him away. James supposed that she was simply too weak, and he tightened his arms about her. "Do you think you can tell me what it is, then?" he whispered against her hair.

Vanessa shook her head silently. James could see that her tears were starting again, and he gently wiped them away. "Please, Vanessa, you know how much I care about you. Won't you tell me what's troubling you?"

Vanessa still didn't answer. James didn't know

what to do. He had an idea that her current distress was somehow connected to her earlier mysterious behavior. *Somehow, in some way, Vanessa has something going on with the earl.* He was desperate to get to the bottom of it, but he wasn't sure just how to broach the subject.

"Vanessa." He took a deep breath. "I have a feeling that this has to do with the earl, doesn't it? Look, no matter how bad it is, you can trust me with your secret."

"No!" Vanessa cried out. She pulled away and looked James in the eye. "I can't tell you! I can't trust you!" She sprang to her feet and began backing away.

"Vanessa . . ." James got to his feet. "Please . . ."

"No!" Vanessa held up a warning hand. "I can't tell you! Leave me alone." She turned and began to run across the lawn. "Just leave me alone!"

"All right," James said unhappily. "I'll leave you alone."

For now, he added silently as he watched her run away.

"Are you crazy?" Bones sounded outraged. "How can you possibly say that Hot Rox is derivative? Their last CD was smashing! Completely original!" He gave Sarah a challenging grin. "Although I agree, the Bloody Young Blokes is a better band."

"I agree with you on that one." Sarah nodded enthusiastically. "Their last single *was* absolutely brilliant." She smiled at him and stretched out across the bed. "Your band rocks out! I like Hot Rox, but I heard some new tunes on the radio, and I think they're starting to lose it. Top up?" She quirked an eyebrow at Bones as she refilled her champagne flute to the brim with Perrier.

"Yes, please." Bones held out his glass as he leaned back against the headboard. "You know a lot about music," he said admiringly. "Most girls only know if they think the guys in a band are hot, but you really know your stuff. I'm impressed."

"Good," Sarah said, reaching for a chocolate truffle. "Here—" She handed Bones a chocolate, then collapsed against the headboard alongside him.

He really is megahot, she thought as she studied him from underneath her lashes. *And a lot of fun too!* So far she'd been having a great time, eating chocolates and chatting with Bones about the current music scene, but Sarah was a little confused as to why he hadn't made a move. *Maybe he really is with Phillipa,* she thought glumly. She finished her truffle and sat up cross-legged, determined to get the truth out of him.

"So how are you finding Welles so far?" she asked casually.

"Hard to tell." Bones shrugged his broad shoulders. "I'm told that it's an absolutely brilliant prep school."

"Who cares about that?" Sarah laughed as she tossed her hair over her shoulder, knowing that the gesture made her look as sexy as possible.

"Well, I do, actually," Bones said to Sarah's intense surprise. "I may be part of a band, and I love that, but another part of me just wants to be a normal sixteen-year-old. I want to play cricket and worry about my marks, not just stress on whether my next single will top the charts. Really, Sarah—" He looked her deeply in the eyes. "You don't know what it's like—everyone thinks I'm so cool, but they like me because I'm famous, not because they really like *me*, if you get what I mean. I hate groupies," he finished glumly.

"But Bones!" Sarah said excitedly. "This is brilliant! I mean, I feel exactly the same way! Oh, I know I'm not famous like you are—" She blushed modestly. "But you'd be surprised how many people suck up to me just because I'm Lady Sarah Pennington."

"Of course." Bones looked at her with interest. "You know exactly what I'm talking about."

I can't believe we have so much in common, Sarah thought as she smiled at Bones. She was amazed at how easy he was to talk to and how funny. *Maybe I*

191

should really try and snag him—and not just to snub Phillipa either—but because he's absolutely fabulous!

"You're right, I do know," Sarah continued, warming to the theme. A flash of inspiration hit her, and she had to hold back a fit of giggles. She knew just how to introduce Phillipa into the conversation—how to introduce her *and* how to demolish her. "In fact, the only people who don't suck up to me are other nobles. *They* get really competitive. Especially the really cowlike ones like Phillipa Ainsley. Of course, I do feel sorry for her and everything because of her little problem. . . ." Sarah trailed off, looking at Bones out of the corner of her eye to see if he was taking the bait.

"Problem? What problem?" Bones frowned. He sipped his Perrier and looked at Sarah with an expectant expression on his face.

"Well." Sarah bit her lip and pretended to look sorry. "It's just so sad to see a girl with so little self-esteem. I mean, I understand *why* she's so insecure, but she should know that sleeping with so many guys *won't* make her feel better. And of course, she did get rather a nasty dose, but sexually transmitted diseases *will* happen when one sleeps around so much."

"Really?" Bones said faintly. He looked absolutely gray, and Sarah was afraid that she was going to burst into laughter. "By the way, I was just wondering." He leaned on his elbow and regarded her with his frank gaze. "Are you actually seeing anyone at the moment?" He sounded casual, but Sarah could see that he was definitely interested.

"Well, no, not right now," Sarah told him. "There was someone a few months ago." She looked him in the eye. "But I'm not really interested in dating, not unless it's someone really special." She lowered her eyelids and leaned a little closer. Their mouths were only inches apart, and she could already taste how good his lips would feel when they kissed. She closed her eyes and waited expectantly.

"Well, that's certainly good to know," Bones said. "Hey, look at the time. I'd better motor. My parents will freak if I'm not home for dinner." He hopped up off the bed.

"Uh, okay." Sarah stared at him, dumbfounded. *Did I miss something?* she wondered. Sarah was sure that he was into her, that she hadn't misread his signals, so what was the problem? "I guess I better get going too," she said quietly as she sat up and slipped on her heels.

"You're a really cool person," Bones said cheerfully as they rode down in the elevator. "I really was just expecting to see Benny."

"I'm glad you were surprised," Sarah murmured,

her mind working furiously. She was going to have to get together with Victoria as soon as possible and work on some serious strategy. One thing was for sure. Now that she'd gotten this close to Bones, she was hooked. There was no way she was giving up until he was hers.

"Well, see you in school." Bones smiled at her as they walked out into the lobby.

"Hmmm. Absolutely. See you," Sarah said absently. Her attention was momentarily distracted by the sight of her brother in the lobby. What was he doing here? And it was a good thing he didn't catch her coming down in the elevator with a guy. He'd have killed her! Then again, given the looks of Max, he probably wouldn't have noticed if she'd come down in her undies. Max was uncharacteristically slumped in one of the lobby chairs. *Gosh, he looks pretty bad!* Sarah felt a brief flash of sympathy. Max did give her a hard time, but she did love him. She didn't want to see him looking so unhappy. *I wonder what the problem is?* Sarah frowned as she exited the opposite way so that he wouldn't see her. *Maybe it's something to do with the human ice sculpture. Maybe I'm not the only one with love troubles!*

"Well, I must say, I am a little peeved," Mary Dale said, frowning as she took a sip of tea. "The earl was courteous enough to announce that he'd be eating in town, and I know that Sarah can be a little flighty, but really, I expected better from Max. Usually they tell us when they won't be home for meals."

What does it mean? Elizabeth wondered as she glanced at the clock. She, along with the rest of the kitchen staff, had been waiting for the past half hour to serve dinner, but so far none of the Penningtons had showed. Elizabeth wasn't so concerned with Sarah's disappearance, but she did wonder why Max hadn't come home.

I guess his tea with Lavinia was so fantastic that he decided to extend it to cocktails, she thought sadly.

"How long do we have to stick around here?" Vanessa asked bluntly. Elizabeth glanced at her curiously. Vanessa still looked terrible. Elizabeth wondered if she was getting sick.

"Might as well let them off now, Mary," Matilda said with a shrug. "My soufflé is ruined, and that's a fact. If Sarah or Max does show up, then they'll just have to make do with toasted cheese," she har-rumphed as she sat down at the table next to Mary.

"I'm afraid we can't very well serve them that," Mary said. "But yes, you're right, we might as well let the girls off early."

"Super!" Alice enthused. She untied her apron

with a grin. "I'm going to take a nice warm bath and go to sleep early."

"I think I might do the same," Vanessa said with considerably less excitement. She moved slowly toward the door.

Well, I'm not ready for bed, Elizabeth thought, looking at the clock again. It was barely six-thirty, and she wanted to make use of the unexpected free time. *What should I do?* She supposed that she could go into London and take in a movie by herself, but the idea wasn't that appealing. She could try to write in her journal again, but that was even less enticing. Elizabeth sighed. What she really wanted to do was have a heart-to-heart with a close girlfriend, someone who would be totally sympathetic about Max and who would take her side entirely, someone who . . . *I know what I'm going to do!* Elizabeth realized suddenly. "Mary—" She turned toward the housekeeper, her eyes sparkling in excitement. "Isn't there a public library around here, and didn't I hear you say that it stayed open late on Wednesday nights?"

"Yes." Mary looked surprised. "It's about a five-minute walk, and it should be open until eight tonight. I suppose you want to get a good mystery or something?"

"Something like that," Elizabeth said with a smile as she headed for the door.

She turned left at the entrance to Pennington House and raced along the pavement as fast as her feet would carry her. Now that her mind was made up, she was impatient to get to the library as fast as possible. *I can't believe I'm doing this!* Elizabeth was amazed at what she was about to do, but she also knew that it had been building for a long time.

Elizabeth rushed up the stairs to the library and presented herself at the main circulation desk. "Hi," she said somewhat breathlessly. "Do you have terminals here where I could get online?"

The librarian looked at her in surprise. *I must look a sight,* Elizabeth realized as she tried to smooth her windblown hair. She took a deep breath and tried again. "Excuse me, do you have computers here where I could get on the Internet? I'm afraid I don't have a library card."

The librarian smiled. "No library card necessary. Our computer is over there—" She pointed to the far corner with her fountain pen. "We just have the one terminal."

"That's all I need." Elizabeth smiled as she headed toward the computer. Her fingers flew over the keyboard as she logged on and began to type her message. *What if Nina doesn't answer?* Elizabeth gnawed at her lower lip anxiously as she thought of what to say in her e-mail. She wanted to pour out her heart, but she thought that she should wait first. Maybe Nina wouldn't want to talk to her—maybe she felt betrayed by Elizabeth's silence all these months. Or maybe she herself had moved. Elizabeth really had no way of knowing. She'd been so cut off from everything, for all she knew, Sweet Valley University had closed down.

Nina—

 Okay, I hope you're sitting down because you're in for a big surprise! Please forgive me for not getting in touch sooner, but things have been kind of crazy for me the last couple of months. (HUGE UNDERSTATEMENT!) I hope that you've been doing well and are into talking to me. I miss you more than you could ever know, and boy, do I have a lot to tell you! Okay, so if you want to talk, e-mail me right back because I don't know when I can get on-line again. I need some serious relationship advice. I'm in love—with the son of an earl, no less, and yes, if you're wondering where I might have run into an earl's son, I'm in London! So please, Nina, write back, and if you're too mad at me, at least don't tell my family where I am. You're the only one who knows!

Love,
Liz

Elizabeth tapped the send key and leaned back with a huge sigh of relief. She'd done it; she'd gotten in touch with someone from back home. Now she just had to see if back home wanted to be in touch with her.

She grew increasingly anxious as the minutes ticked by. What if Nina ignored her plea and told Jessica where she was? Elizabeth might be ready to talk to Nina, but she wasn't ready to talk to Jessica—no matter how much she might be missing her lately. What if Nina really wanted to talk to her, but she didn't get the e-mail until tomorrow?

I guess I can always . . . Elizabeth sat up in excitement. Someone had just sent her a message. She double clicked on it eagerly.

> *Where've you been, girl?! I am so glad to hear from you! I was worried sick about you!*

Elizabeth felt tears welling up as she read Nina's message. It felt so good to hear from her that Elizabeth wondered why she'd denied herself the pleasure for so long.

> *Trust you to land someone wildly eligible! Tell all! I'm dying of curiosity about everything, Elizabeth, and I'm not just talking about the new guy. But you can start*

with him and backtrack when you want to.
I'll be hanging at the computer, just waiting
for you to write back! Is he cute? Is he rich?
Is he older? C'mon, spill!

Love,
Nina

Elizabeth laughed through her tears as she typed her next message and settled in for a long chat.

Chapter
Eleven

The gentle sound of the rain as it pattered on the roof woke Elizabeth up early on Thursday morning. Vanessa and Alice were still asleep, and she lay on her back, luxuriating in the few moments of privacy allowed her before the day's chores began.

Elizabeth hugged her pillow close as she remembered the events of the evening before. *It felt so good to talk to Nina,* she thought, tears springing to her eyes. She wiped them away with the back of her hand. *Why am I so weepy?* Elizabeth asked herself. Things were going well. *I finally have someone to talk to again—even if she is over five thousand miles away!* Now that she'd made the first step, she knew she could count on Nina to e-mail her regularly. So why was she feeling so down?

Elizabeth reached under her bed for her journal. Maybe a little early morning writing would help her sort through whatever was bothering her. After making sure that Vanessa and Alice were still sleeping, she flipped open the book.

Of course! Elizabeth gasped as she looked at the date. How could she have forgotten already? She knew that Thanksgiving was coming, and she'd expected it to be hard, but still, now that the day had actually arrived, she felt worse than she could possibly have imagined.

Elizabeth lay back down and closed her eyes. Memories of past years swept over her—Jessica being scolded for feeding Prince Albert, who was still a puppy, scraps under the table. She pictured her father saying grace and her mother serving the turkey on *her* mother's prized china. Laughter mixed with tears as she recalled the time that Steven had wanted to impress a girl and baked the pumpkin pie himself—the only problem was that he mixed up the sugar and salt canisters, and the resulting pie had been completely inedible.

What is everybody doing now? Elizabeth wondered. *I guess they're still asleep.* She half smiled. But in a few hours they'd be preparing dinner. Jessica would be arguing with Steven over how much sage to put in the stuffing. Her mother would put them both to work polishing the silver, just like Mary with Vanessa. Elizabeth chuckled. *Next year I'll really be able to whiz through that silver!* Her expression sobered. Would she be there next year? Surely she wouldn't still be estranged from her parents by then—would she?

But do I want to see them? she asked herself. *And if I am back there next year, then does that mean I won't see Max again?* Elizabeth shook her head in dismay. She didn't know what the future held. She knew that she wasn't going to be a scullery maid forever, but beyond that, whether she got in touch with her parents again or where Max fit in, she just didn't know.

Too many questions . . . I can't think about such life-or-death matters right now. I just have to get through the day.

"Elizabeth!" Vanessa's sharp voice sliced through her thoughts like a knife. "Are you trying to figure out how to arrange peace in the Mideast or something—or did dinner not agree with you? You've got the most ghastly expression on your face."

Elizabeth rolled over on her side and faced Vanessa. "Whatever happened to a simple good morning?" she asked mildly. God, but sometimes Vanessa's moods were tiresome.

"Good morning," Alice piped up from the other bed.

"Hey, good morning." Elizabeth turned and smiled at her.

"Well, if you two aren't going to use the loo, then I will." Vanessa leaped out of bed and pranced off to the bathroom.

Elizabeth glanced at the clock; it was still quite early. She could go down, have her own breakfast, come up and shower, and still be early for the morning breakfast prep. She jumped out of bed and grabbed a pair of jeans from the closet that they shared. She could put on her uniform after she showered.

"I'll catch up with you later, Alice," Elizabeth said, smiling again at the huddled form underneath mountains of blankets as she dragged a comb through her hair. "I'm going to grab some breakfast."

Elizabeth headed downstairs and pushed into the kitchen.

"You're up early," Mary said.

"I couldn't fall back to sleep," Elizabeth replied with a shrug.

"Well, as long as you're here, you can taste the scones. They're fresh out of the oven, but it's a new recipe, and Matilda isn't sure they're quite right."

"I'd be honored to be your taste tester, Matilda." Elizabeth smiled at the cook. "But I'm certain that they're delicious."

"I don't know." Matilda looked concerned as she took a baking sheet out of the oven. "With that a new recipe, I have my doubts. Sarah likes her chocolate scones, and the earl is fond of raisin. What they'll make of cranberries is anybody's guess."

"Cranberries!" Elizabeth exclaimed. All the feelings that she'd been trying to suppress threatened to overwhelm her.

"Are you allergic?" Matilda frowned.

Elizabeth shook her head wordlessly. How could she explain to them what was going on with her without breaking down in tears? As strict as Mary and Matilda were, Elizabeth knew that they could also be kind, but she didn't want to burden them with her feelings.

"Something tells me that Elizabeth is having a different kind of reaction." Mary regarded her shrewdly. She got up and walked over to the wall calendar. "Today's Thanksgiving, isn't it? And cranberries are some kind of national dish, aren't they?"

"Y-Yes," Elizabeth stammered.

"Well." Mary considered for a moment. "We're not fearfully busy here today. The earl's lunching in town, and there isn't anything special planned for dinner. I know how important Thanksgiving is to Americans. You're a hard worker, Elizabeth, and if you want to have the day off, you may take it."

"Thank you!" Elizabeth exclaimed in surprise. So Mary wasn't such a beast after all. *Let's see, what should I do with a free day?* she wondered. *Be depressed about my family situation? Be depressed about the Max situation?* She sighed. Some day off.

London. She'd go into town and have her own little celebration. Maybe she'd go to one of the museums, or maybe she'd take herself out to one of the high teas that she was always serving to the earl and his family but had never had the occasion to taste.

I'll wear something nice too—maybe that will help cheer me up, she thought as she headed out of the kitchen.

"Elizabeth!" Matilda called out.

"Yes?" Elizabeth whirled around. Was there some chore that Matilda would want her to do first?

"Here, poppet." She handed Elizabeth one of the still warm, fragrant cranberry scones. "If you can't be with your family and friends today, you can at least have some cranberries."

Elizabeth felt her heart squeeze. "Thank you. Thanks a lot." She took a giant bite of the scone as she raced up the stairs, already planning what she would wear on her outing.

Max swerved sharply, barely missing a mailbox as he pushed the Jaguar to its maximum speed limit. *Bloody hell! That just popped up out of nowhere,* he thought as he floored the accelerator.

He knew that his reflexes were off—after all, he'd barely slept a wink all night—and that he shouldn't be driving so quickly, but he couldn't help it. He had to get to Lavinia's as soon as possible.

I've got to find out what she was on about yesterday, he thought, frowning as the countryside flew by the window. *What scandal was she talking about, and how does she know?* Max turned onto the road that led to Lavinia's estate, his mind a mass of questions. Had she possibly been making the whole thing up? Was it a spur-of-the-moment thing? A reaction to his own cruel confession?

Maybe that's it, he thought, nodding as he pulled into the circular drive. *She was just lashing out at me because I hurt her so badly.* Max hoped with all his heart that would prove to be the case. If Lavinia *was* telling the truth—well, then he was in a bind. There was simply no way he'd end his engagement if it meant that his sister would be affected as seriously as Lavinia had hinted she would be.

But if she was making the whole thing up . . . Max hardly dared allow himself to hope. If she was making the whole thing up, then he would consider himself free to truly end things with Lavinia and pursue his own hopes and dreams.

Max slammed the car door and sprinted up the

steps. He didn't even have time to ring before the door was opened by Lavinia herself. He blinked in surprise. Lavinia answering the door? That was unusual; had she been watching for him? She appeared as self-possessed and perfect as always, and as always she was perfectly turned out—today she was wearing a pale blue dress that exactly matched her eyes. But as Max looked closer, he was sure that he saw the telltale traces of tears beneath the carefully applied eye makeup, and her face was as ghostly pale as it had been the day before.

"Max." Her voice was cool as she stepped back to let him in. "To what do I owe this pleasant surprise? We'll take tea in the drawing room, Joseph," she said, turning to her majordomo. "This way." She smiled briefly at Max.

Her heels clicked over the marble floor as she led the way to the drawing room. "That will do, Marie," she said to the maid, who was busy dusting a pair of priceless eighteenth-century figurines.

"Well—" Lavinia turned back to Max as she settled herself on a small love seat and crossed one elegant leg over the other. "Should I take this as a sign that you're willing to talk about the éclairs at last, or are you going to make another declaration of love for the American maid?"

"You bloody well know what I've come to talk about," Max said through clenched teeth. He lowered himself onto a small slipper chair across from the love seat and glared at her.

"Hmmm, no, actually, I really don't." Lavinia looked bored as she studied her nails. She seemed extremely nonchalant, but Max had the distinct feeling that she was putting on an act for his benefit.

"Spare me the game playing, Lavinia," he said, glaring at her. "You owe me an explanation for yesterday."

"Oh, really?" Lavinia raised an eyebrow. "Are you sure that you have that right, Max? I'm afraid I see things a little differently." She leaned forward and clasped her knees. "You see, from my perspective *you* owe *me* an explanation for yesterday. After all, it's not every day that one's fiancé announces that he's in love with another girl." Her voice faltered a little, but she recovered herself and flashed an icy smile at Max.

She's right. Max bowed his head in shame, but he couldn't help feeling a brief surge of hope. Clearly Lavinia was hurting more than she was willing to let on. Would the pain that he'd inflicted on her spur her to vengeance? *Had* she been lying about the scandal that haunted his family?

"For whatever pain I've caused you, Lavinia—" He raised his head and looked deep into her eyes.

209

"I'm profoundly sorry. The last thing that I ever wanted to do was hurt you."

"Oh, spare me the cheap sentiment," Lavinia said, dismissing his apology with a wave of her perfectly manicured hand. "It's about as touching, *and* convincing, as your avowals of undying love for the little scullery maid." She paused as Joseph came into the room, bearing a silver tea tray. "Right there if you would, Joseph." Lavinia indicated a small table next to the love seat.

"So, you were saying?" She raised an eyebrow at Max as she moved to pour the tea. "Cream and sugar?"

"Neither, thank you," Max said tightly. *This is so absurd,* he thought as he watched Lavinia cut a slice of pound cake and place it on a small dish along with several miniature scones. *I'm trying to end our engagement, and she's playing tea party!*

"Perhaps you don't take my sentiments very seriously," Max said quietly. "But Lavinia, take this seriously. I will not leave this house unless you divulge everything about this so-called family scandal that you seemed to have drummed up out of thin air."

"Really, Max." Lavinia took a sip of her tea, then leaned forward to stir in another teaspoon of sugar. "Has anyone ever told you that you talk like a character in a Victorian novel? Honestly, if I had a brother, you'd be challenging him to a duel."

"I mean it, Lavinia." Max knotted his fists in frustration. "Unless you start telling me the details of this so-called scandal, I'm going to conclude that you made the whole thing up, and I won't think twice about calling off our engagement."

"I wouldn't be so hasty if I were you, Max." Lavinia placed her teacup down with exaggerated care and looked him directly in the eye. "I can assure you if you call off our engagement, I'll leak this scandal, which is most definitely real, to the press. I doubt there's a single decent family in the kingdom who'll receive you after I do. And you can forget about Sarah's chances for any kind of a future."

"What in blazes is this scandal?" Max was white with fury.

"Hmmm." Lavinia steepled her hands together and regarded Max with a shrewd expression. "How shall I say this? Your father's a very attractive man, Max—did you ever wonder if your mother was his only love?"

"What are you talking about?" Max asked as a cold finger of fear snaked its way down his spine.

"Well, what if I told you that he had an affair?" Lavinia took a delicate bite of the pound cake.

"I'd say that was rubbish." Max wouldn't believe it. He wouldn't. He picked up the teacup more to have something to do with his hands than because he was thirsty.

"Well," Lavinia went on. "What if I told you that your father didn't just have a relationship with another woman; what if I told you that he also had a child by that woman?"

"What?" Max cried out in astonishment. He dropped his cup, and the priceless Wedgwood shattered into a thousand pieces against the herringbone mahogany floor.

"Don't worry about it, Joseph," Lavinia said as the majordomo poked his head around the door. "You can send Marie in to deal with it later."

"Well, Max." Lavinia turned back to him. "Is that scandal enough for you?"

"You're bluffing," Max sputtered. "You're making the whole thing up—it's absolutely impossible."

"Is it?" Lavinia sounded dubious. "I don't think so, considering that my own mother told me about it. And you know how close my parents were with the earl and your mother. So tell me, Max, how does it feel to realize that you have another sibling out there?"

"I don't have another sibling!" Max insisted. He paced back and forth like a caged lion. "It just can't be true!"

"Oh, I think you know that it *can* be," Lavinia drawled. "You just don't *want* it to be—there's a difference."

"You're bluffing." Max spun on his heel and

pointed an accusing finger at Lavinia. "You know bloody well that my father never had an illegitimate child. This whole thing is a pathetic ploy to hang on to me. Well, forget it, Lavinia, I'm not buying it. The wedding's off." He moved toward the door.

"If you call off the wedding, Max—" Lavinia's voice was positively glacial. "Then I will be forced to play my hand and leak this story to the press. Think of it, Max. Page one. It won't be pretty. Imagine how poor Sarah will feel when everyone starts to shun her at Welles. Imagine how your father will feel when the reporters descend on Pennington House."

"You have the upper hand now, Lavinia," Max said, turning to face her once more. "But don't think that I'm going to leave things like this. If I find out that you've made this up . . ." He left his threat unspoken as he slammed the door behind him and raced out of the house.

What now? Max thought as he slid behind the wheel of the Jaguar. While he didn't mind any scandal that might attach itself to his own name, he would do anything to prevent his father and Sarah from being hurt. Anything. Even marrying Lavinia.

Max barely knew where he was headed as he turned the car toward London. He only knew that he didn't want to go home. He didn't want to look his father in the face and wonder about Lavinia's accusations.

The traffic in Piccadilly Circus was murder, and he decided to park the car and wander around on foot. *Maybe I can figure out some way of finding out if there's any truth to all this,* he thought as he swung into the garage that he used whenever he was in town.

It was just starting to rain as Max struck out on foot, and he decided to duck into a store and wait out the worst of it before heading on. Luckily Hatchards was only a few minutes' walk.

I never imagined that this sort of thing could happen, he thought sadly as he pushed open the door. *I thought that as long as I was—* "Elizabeth!" Max gasped. There, standing in the bookstore and looking like an angel, was the object of all his desires and the recipient of all his silent longings. He vowed to forget Lavinia and the scandal she was threatening him with, at least for this one afternoon. Yes. Today he would take for himself, for Elizabeth. Tomorrow he'd deal with the hell awaiting him.

Vanessa paced back and forth nervously. Her feet sank soundlessly into the lush pile of the ancient Persian runner that covered the entire length of the hall outside the earl's study as she flicked at the oil paintings with her dust cloth.

She had no desire to dust the pictures of his grotty ancestors, but she needed some activity so that she wouldn't look suspicious if Mary or one of the

214

girls happened by. Vanessa should have finished with the upstairs hallway long ago, but she wasn't about to leave, not until the earl showed up and she could confront him with the pictures and the letter that had been burning a hole in her pocket for the past day.

She was startled by a sudden sound and whirled around, expecting to see the earl. No one was there, however, and she exhaled shakily. *Stop being so nervous!* she chided herself. *He's the guilty one, not you!*

Vanessa closed her eyes and mentally prepared for the scene she was about to enact. She'd been over it a thousand times since she'd found the love note, but she still wasn't sure just how she wanted to confront the earl.

Should she be completely silent and proud and simply hand him the pictures? Should she throw them in his face and scream at him? A dose of hysteria would be a change from the stiff-upper-lip behavior he was used to. Of course, just having a servant talk to him in the first place would probably be enough to send him into cardiac arrest. But what approach would shock him the most? What approach would hurt him the most?

Vanessa paused for a second and cocked her head. This time there *was* a noise. Someone was coming down the hallway. She took a deep breath and shored up her courage for the battle ahead.

What the bloody . . . Vanessa stared openmouthed

as the earl and a well-known member of Parliament strolled down the hall toward her. Her knees felt weak as she imagined the scene that would ensue if she played her hand in front of the MP.

On the one hand, if she accosted the earl now, in front of his colleague, she'd be almost sure to ruin his career in a single swift stroke. But on the other hand . . . Vanessa was nervous enough about tackling the earl; did she really have the strength to deal with *two* of them? She stood frozen as the earl came closer. He was deep in conversation with his associate, but he glanced at Vanessa in surprise as he paused to unlock his study.

"Why are you hanging about here?" he asked roughly. "Shouldn't you be in the kitchen?"

Vanessa could feel her face turning fiery red. How dare he speak to her in that tone? *You wouldn't be that dismissive if you knew who I really was,* she thought as she reached into her apron pocket for the pictures.

"And see to it that the Gainsborough at the end of the hall is dusted—I see a film on it," he added, nodding toward one of the more famous paintings before entering his study and slamming the door behind him.

Foiled! Vanessa was amazed at how quickly he'd moved. She'd lost her opportunity!

Don't be silly, she told herself. *I haven't lost my opportunity. His time will come, and come soon too, I promise.*

She turned and flounced off downstairs, making sure to throw her dust cloth at the Gainsborough on the way.

"Well, what's your pleasure?" Max asked Elizabeth as they walked through Piccadilly.

"Anything," Elizabeth said, smiling. It was true too. As long as she was with Max, she didn't care what they did or where they went.

She'd been surprised to see him in the bookstore, but surprise had quickly given way to pleasure when it became clear that he wanted to spend the day with her. Max had assured her that there was nothing he wanted more than to show her London, and Elizabeth had happily agreed. Of course her mind was teeming with questions about Lavinia, but she pushed them firmly aside as she prepared to enjoy the day.

It's just like a regular old date! Elizabeth thought happily as she quickened her pace so that she could keep up with him. Although her date seemed very preoccupied. She wondered what happened last night. And when he was going to talk to her about whatever it was he'd brought up yesterday.

"By the way, have I told you how lovely you look?" Max asked. "I think this is the first time I've seen you out of the Pennington House staff uniform."

"That's probably true," Elizabeth said, laughing.

She was glad that she'd made the effort to look her best. Although her wardrobe wasn't extensive, she'd picked up a few things since she'd been in London, and today she was wearing an extra-flattering pair of jeans with a hand-crocheted sweater that she'd gotten in the Portobello market.

"Well, back to the main question," Max said. "What shall we do? The National Gallery? The Tate? Tea at Harrods, or how about a simple pub lunch at my favorite place?"

"Any and all of them," Elizabeth said. "I'm just happy to be with you," she added shyly.

"I feel the same way." Max squeezed her hand. He stopped walking and looked down at her with an intent expression on his handsome face. "Elizabeth, can we just spend the day as if we really were together? I mean—" He blushed slightly. "As if there were no Lavinia, no other obligations, no other pressures, as if there were only us."

Elizabeth was speechless. She reached up and kissed him quickly on the cheek.

"I take it that means yes." Max's smile widened. "Look, it's almost lunchtime. Why don't we stop off in a pub, unless you want something a little fancier, and get something to eat?"

"A pub sounds wonderful," Elizabeth said as they threaded their way through the crowded streets. "Although a real English tea sounds nice

218

too. You know, in the five months that I've been here, I've never had one!"

"Impossible! You've been in England that long and never downed one single, stodgy, fattening high tea?" Max laughed.

"Hmmm, well, when you put it that way, I'm not sure that I want one after all." Elizabeth grinned. She looked up as they passed one of the famous Piccadilly monuments. *I saw that on my first day here!* Elizabeth realized. It seemed incredible that she'd come so far. That first day she wasn't sure she was going to make it. Now she was walking hand in hand with one of the most wonderful guys in all of England. *I certainly landed on my feet,* she couldn't help thinking.

"Is something wrong?" Max looked confused. "You just sighed so deeply—was it something I said?" He led her off the main drag and onto a side street. "Why don't we sit down for a second and you can tell me what's on your mind." He walked toward a small square, planted with late-blooming roses and with a wrought-iron bench in the middle.

"Absolutely nothing's wrong." Elizabeth shook her head vehemently. "In fact, I was just thinking about how well things have turned out for me this year." She sat down on the bench and snuggled closer to Max as he draped an arm casually around her shoulders. "I told you about my problems the other day," she continued. "How I was running away. But look at me now—I'm in one of the most exciting cities in the world, with one of the most exciting men."

Max leaned forward and plucked a rose from one of the bushes, then carefully removed the thorns and handed the blossom to Elizabeth. "I don't know if you're with one of the most exciting men," he said, brushing a tendril of hair off her face. "But I do know that I'm with one of the most exciting, beautiful, brave women in the world. Elizabeth, if things were different, if Lav—"

"Shhh." Elizabeth placed her hand against his mouth to cut off his words. She thrilled at the feel of his warm breath against her palm. "We said that we wouldn't talk about Lav—" She checked herself. "About things like that," she finished.

Max was silent, but he took Elizabeth's hand away from his mouth and smothered it in kisses. Elizabeth closed her eyes and allowed the delicious sensations he was arousing to wash over her. "Elizabeth," Max murmured between kisses. "You're right, of course, but I can't help feeling sad. I want to be with you—for a long while—and in many ways I feel like we belong together, but our time together is so limited."

"Then let's make the most of it," Elizabeth said softly. She withdrew her hand and wrapped both her arms about his neck. "Let's make the most of it," she repeated as she leaned in to kiss him.

"Now what?" Max said when he came up for air. "Although I would like to stay here and kiss you all day, it is starting to rain, so we should probably come up with some sort of plan."

"You call this rain?" Elizabeth gestured at the slight drizzle. "And you call yourself an Englishman! Even I can handle rain like this, and I'm from southern California!"

"Well, at least I've had a few thousand high teas," Max joked. "No, look." He got up and swung Elizabeth to her feet. "We really should make sure you have one. You really can't say that you've been to England unless you've tried at least one."

"But they don't usually serve them until much later on in the afternoon, do they?" Elizabeth asked as they left the secluded square and headed toward one of the busier streets.

"Hmmm, true enough." Max frowned. "Look, I know what we'll do. It's nearly lunchtime, so why don't we duck into a pub, then we'll pop into one of the museums. I think you might like the National; in any case, it's quite near here. Museums always make me hungry—does that happen to you too?"

"Actually, they wear my feet out," Elizabeth admitted.

"Well, okay, you'll be ready for a break, then. That's when we'll have our tea."

"Sounds good to me." Elizabeth smiled as she followed him into a pub. "Wow!" She waved a hand in front of her face. "Now I know I'm not in California anymore! Don't they have no-smoking laws in this country?"

"Are you kidding?" Max grinned at her as he slid into one of the red leather booths. "Smoking in pubs is practically a national sport. Does it bother you?" He looked concerned.

"No, it's fine." Elizabeth flipped open her menu. "What's a ploughman's lunch?" She frowned.

"Best avoided," Max said firmly. "Roast-beef sandwiches are the way to go here—those and darts are the best thing on offer." He waved his hand at a large dartboard on the opposite wall.

Elizabeth stared at the dartboard. The first thought that ran through her mind was that Sam used to play darts at every opportunity. The second was that thinking of Sam didn't even bother her. *I guess that means I'm truly ready to move on,* she thought as she turned back to face Max. *And Max is the one that I'm ready to move on with!*

Chapter Twelve

Vanessa's legs felt so shaky that she could barely walk down the hall. Her heart was in her throat, and beads of sweat gathered on her forehead.

I'm finally going to confront the earl! Her knees trembled as she approached his office. Vanessa had been waiting anxiously all day for the right moment, and when she'd heard the earl tell Mary that he was going to be alone in his study after dinner, she knew that the time had finally come.

You can do it! Vanessa told herself fiercely. She'd imagined this moment for so many months now. She'd seen herself victorious, triumphant, successful. But never, never had she imagined that she'd be so scared.

She paused outside the door to his study, her heart thumping so wildly that she was surprised he couldn't hear it through the thick mahogany door.

Why are you so scared, girl? she chastised herself. *He's the one who should be scared! He's the one who's done something wrong!*

Vanessa took a deep breath as she raised her hand to knock against the door.

"Who is it?" the earl called out.

Vanessa couldn't bring herself to answer. She simply knocked again, this time a little more forcefully.

"I said, who is it?" The earl yanked open the door and thrust out his head. It was obvious that he was highly irritated at being interrupted. "Oh, it's you." He frowned as he looked at Vanessa. "I didn't order anything from the kitchen."

Vanessa knew that she should tell him that she was his daughter. She knew that she should accuse him of ruining her mother's life, but she couldn't say a word. She just stood still and stared at him. *This man's my father, this man's my father.* The words kept repeating themselves in her head.

"I told you, I didn't order anything," the earl said briskly. "Now run off to the kitchen."

Vanessa stared at him, her mouth curled in contempt. How dare he talk to her that way! Without thinking what she was doing, she reached into her apron pocket and thrust one picture of himself and her mother, embracing, in his face.

The earl turned a deadly shade of white.

*   *   *

224

Elizabeth hummed a little tune as she stood in front of her bathroom mirror, brushing out her hair. She couldn't remember the last time that she'd felt this happy. She and Max had spent one of the most fabulous, thrilling, exciting days that she'd ever had. After eating lunch in the pub, they'd gone to the National Gallery and wandered around, drinking in the great paintings. Then they'd walked across London to Brown's, which, according to Max, was one of the most sophisticated hotels in the city. They'd ordered an absolutely sumptuous high tea, Elizabeth had positively lapped up the clotted cream, and then they'd taken a leisurely walk back to where Max was parked. Instead of driving home, Max had taken her to Epping Forest, where they'd stopped and kissed for what seemed like hours.

I don't think I've ever felt like this. Elizabeth leaned into the mirror to study her face. She still looked flushed, as if she and Max had just stopped kissing. *Maybe that's because I can't stop thinking about it,* she thought, smiling.

She knew he wasn't hers. She knew she had to give him up. And she knew that what they were doing was wrong, no matter what the circumstances. But she was in love. And that felt so right. So, so right.

"Elizabeth?" Alice poked her head around the

225

door. "Max is on the house phone. He said he must speak to you. It's urgent."

Max? Elizabeth hurried out of the bathroom and picked up the house extension that stood on a little table next to her bed.

"Max?" she asked hesitantly. Was he calling to say good night, perhaps? She couldn't imagine that he would do such a thing.

"Elizabeth, look, I hate to bother you. But I absolutely must talk to you. Could you come to my room? Tell the other girls that I've had a Häagen-Dazs attack and that I said you had to serve it. Tell them whatever you want, but tell them something. I need to see you."

"Of course," Elizabeth murmured. She put down the phone and raced down the hall toward the back stairs.

When she reached his door, she glanced to the left and right to make sure no one would see her enter. She opened the door and slipped inside.

"Elizabeth." Max held out his arms.

Elizabeth went to him. "Max, what is it, what happened?" she asked, loving the way the slight stubble on his cheek felt against hers.

"We need to talk." Max led her over to his bed, where they both sat down. "Elizabeth, today was one of the most wonderful days of my life. I

226

can't remember the last time I felt that good."

"I was just thinking the same thing," Elizabeth said simply. She held tightly on to Max's hand as if it were a lifeline.

"Elizabeth," Max said, turning so that he was looking straight at her. "I love you. I didn't want to tell you, I didn't even want to admit it to my-self—it would be so much simpler if I didn't. But I do. I love you, Elizabeth."

"Oh, Max." Elizabeth was overcome. "You must know that I love you too."

"Elizabeth." Max kissed her. "I want to leave Lavinia."

Elizabeth's heart did a somersault. His wanting to leave Lavinia was almost as thrilling as his telling her that he loved her.

"But I can't," he continued as he got up off the bed and began pacing back and forth across the room. "I went to tell her that today, well, yes-terday, actually," he said, running his hand through his hair. "To say it didn't go over too well would be an insane understatement."

"What happened?" Elizabeth asked, her heart in her throat. She felt like her whole future de-pended on his answer.

"She threatened me," Max said simply. He looked at Elizabeth with a bleak expression on his face. "She threatened me," he repeated.

227

"How," Elizabeth faltered. "Is she . . . is she pregnant, Max, is that it?"

"If she is, it's not by me," Max said angrily. "We never slept together, Elizabeth."

"I'm glad," Elizabeth said honestly. "You don't know how glad I am to hear that. But what did she threaten you with?" She frowned. "I mean, there isn't some deep, dark secret hanging over your past, is there?" She tried to sound light-hearted, but it came out flat.

"Apparently there is," Max said grimly. He knelt at the foot of the bed and grasped her hands. "Lavinia says that there's a terrible scandal involving my father and that if I call off the engagement, she'll go to the press. It could mean my father's ruin." He tightened his grip on her hands. "It would kill him, Elizabeth, it really would."

"My God!" Elizabeth's eyes widened. "I can't believe she would do something so devious."

"Lavinia is a bit power mad," Max said sadly. "She sees our marriage as a business merger, one that she won't let go of without a fight."

"But Max, maybe she's bluffing!"

"Then it's a bluff I'm much too afraid to call," Max said, closing his eyes. "Oh, Elizabeth." He rested his head on her lap. "I'd give anything to be with you. I'd let my name be dragged through the mud and never think twice, but I can't bring about my father's ruin or my sister's. It's Sarah who Lavinia says will suffer the most because of the scandal. I can't risk it, Elizabeth. I just can't."

"I understand, Max," Elizabeth said in a voice thick with tears as she stroked his hair. "I do understand," she repeated as the teardrops slid down her face and onto his hair.

"Don't cry, Elizabeth," Max said, looking at her. "Don't cry, because if you do, then I will, and I won't be able to stop."

Elizabeth shook her head, but the tears continued to fall. She loved Max so much—*and he loves me!* Why did things have to be this way? Why did life have to be so unfair? All Elizabeth wanted was to love Max and be loved in return. Why did they need this hideous impediment? She knew that she would never have him. That Lavinia, with her ugly threats, whatever they were, had won. Max would marry her and have a loveless marriage, and Elizabeth would always dream of what might have been.

But we do have tonight, she realized with crystal clarity. They could have this one night, and no one would ever be able to take it away from them.

I want to make love with Max, Elizabeth realized with stunning clarity. She wanted a night to remember always. Slowly she got up from the bed.

"Elizabeth?" Max looked at her questioningly.

Elizabeth didn't say anything. Slowly she took off her top and her jeans. She stood in her white lacy underwear, gazing at Max, gazing at the guy she loved with all her heart.

"Elizabeth?" Max looked at her like she was a goddess and he could hardly believe that she was real. "Are you sure?" he asked quietly.

Elizabeth nodded. She had never felt so sure of anything in her life.

Max stood and gathered her close and rained kisses down on her face. "Elizabeth, Elizabeth," he murmured against the silk of her hair. "I do love you so much."

Elizabeth returned his kisses, her heart never bigger, never fuller.

Elizabeth lay with her head on Max's chest as he lazily stroked her hair. She'd never felt so at peace with the world. She wanted to stay there forever, but already the dawn was breaking and the first glimmers of sunlight were streaming through the curtains.

"That was your first time, wasn't it?" Max asked softly as he continued stroking her hair.

"Yes," Elizabeth whispered against his chest. "It was."

"I'm so glad it was with me," Max murmured in an awed voice. "I love you, Elizabeth."

"I love you too," Elizabeth said dreamily. Making love with Max was everything she had ever imagined it would be. "What are we going to do now?"

"I don't know." Max's voice was gruff. "I don't have the answers, Elizabeth, but I do know that I can't bear to be parted from you. Not now. Not ever."

"I feel the same way," Elizabeth answered sleepily. She knew that she wanted to be with Max, and she knew that he was bound more than ever to Lavinia. But she didn't care because she was sure that a love as strong and pure as theirs would triumph. It had to. There was simply no other outcome that she would accept.

"We'll figure something out," Max said, echoing her thoughts. "We have to. That's all there is to it."

Elizabeth smiled drowsily as she held on to Max. She felt like she had turned a corner. She was her own person.

Watch out, Lavinia, Elizabeth vowed. *You haven't had the last word yet! And you never will either, not if I have anything to say about it!*